Stranger in the Mirror

By Jim Kruger

Copyright © 2002 by Jim Kruger

ISBN 978-0-7414-0951-5

Published by:

INFINITY PUBLISHING

Toll-free (877) BUY BOOK
Local Phone (610) 941-9999
Fax (610) 941-9959
Info@buybooksontheweb.com
www.buybooksontheweb.com

Printed in the United States of America

Published November, 2012

Chapter 1

The flash came first, a blinding flash, followed by a deafening explosion that lifted me up and slammed me down into unconsciousness. It was the cold that finally brought me around. I was lying face down in the snow and I was numb all over. When I tried to lift my head blood ran into my eyes and the numbness turned to excruciating pain. I'd been hit and I knew I was out of the fight, maybe for good. Nothing much registered but the pain that pulsated in waves of light and darkness. I was bleeding badly and there wasn't a damn thing I could about it. A helluva place to die, I thought. But where was I? Must be a cliff, because I seemed to be slipping slowly over the edge with nothing to grab but a handful of bloody snow. As I plunged toward black eternity I heard the blare of bugles, the shouting of desperate men and the thunderous roar of artillery exploding all around amid the crackle of small arms fire. Then I felt fingers on my throat, gentle fingers, groping for a pulse. I smelled perfume mingled with gun smoke.

"Is he dead?" a man asked.

"No," a woman's voice replied. "How's the other one?"

"Blown away."

"We can come back for him. Let's get this one back down."

That was it. That was all I could remember when I woke up in a strange bed in a rustic cabin that smelled of pine smoke. I was buried in quilts and logs blazed in the fireplace. My head was splitting. It hurt just to open my eyes. Outside a truck engine revved up and idled briefly with a deep rumble. Then tires crunched over loose gravel and faded into the distance. The door opened quietly and a woman entered the room, a tall woman with gorgeous red hair that hung to

1

her shoulders. She leaned close, studying me carefully. She had beautiful blue eyes.

"How are you feeling?"

"Like that truck has been parked on my head."

She smiled and reached tentatively for my bandaged head. It was a comforting move, a motherly gesture. She checked the bandage carefully and I figured this was the same touch I'd felt out there in the snow. Then I caught a whiff of her perfume and I was sure of it.

"Help me up, will you?"

"All right, but take it easy. Here, put your arm around my shoulder. The doctor says no fast moves, no exertion, no excitement. You've had your bell rung pretty good."

She got me up and into a robe and across a cold floor into the bathroom. I may have remembered the smell of her perfume, but I couldn't place the face that looked back at me from the mirror. Whatever it was that smacked me had lifted a piece of my scalp just at the hairline. It hurt when I touched the bandage that covered my head like a bowl. There was gray hair sticking out from under it. The stubble of beard on my chin was gray, too. If I wasn't an old man before I got hit, I sure as hell was now. The face had a lot of years on it, a lot of hard years judging from the wrinkles. It didn't help that my eyes were black and swollen nearly shut, like I'd just gone ten rounds with the reigning heavyweight. Who was the reigning heavyweight? I must have left my memory back there in the snow, because the P.M. monogram on my robe didn't ring any bells either. I figured the redhead could tell me who and where I am, but I decided to play it cool until I got my bearings. She was straightening out the bed when I came out.

"How long have I been here?" I asked.

"A day and a half. We brought you down right away after we found you."

"Brought me down?"

"The two of you were about a mile up the canyon when I heard the shots. I got there as soon as I could and Bob and I brought you down."

"You said the two of us…"

"Frank's dead."

I remember from those few moments in the snow that someone was dead, but the name Frank didn't tell me anything. It must have been my blank look that made her suspicious.

"You don't remember much, do you?"

"In all fairness, I took quite a thump."

"You had your hair parted by a slug from a thirty-aught-six. Just how much *do* you remember?"

There was no playing it cool with this one. She was tough and sharp and she was pumping me.

"I don't remember a thing. I don't know where I am or what I'm doing here or how I got thumped. And I don't remember you, but it's nothing personal. I don't remember me, either."

"You mean you've got amnesia?" There was a note of skepticism in her voice.

"I guess that's what they call it. So let's put it together. You start from the top and if the tune sounds familiar I'll chime in."

"For openers, you're at Campbell Lodge," she said, somewhat impatiently. "You and Frank Carter arrived about a week ago from the outside. It's rained most of the time, but day before yesterday it cleared and we packed up and got on the trail after caribou. Bob – he's my husband – drove us to the trailhead and the three of us set out on foot. I picked up caribou tracks in the fresh snow and we followed them until we spotted a buck on a ledge about a hundred yards above us. I headed back to the truck for a scope and on the way I heard two shots so close together they sounded like one. I ran back and found both of you lying in the snow. Frank was dead. Your scalp was ripped open and you were bleeding like crazy. Bob came running up the trail then and tried to

3

stop the bleeding. We used the game sling to carry you back to the truck, brought you down here to the lodge and called the doctor. He patched you up and called the sheriff. Bob and the sheriff just left to pick up what's left of Frank."

"I guess that sheriff will have a some questions for me when he gets back."

"I imagine he will."

She threw another log on the fire and left for the lodge to fix me a tray. It was raining and I watched her through the window as she ran the thirty yards to the main building, an odd looking structure for a hunting lodge. It had a small steeple or belfry at one end. She was a tall, big-boned woman, but a very attractive one, well rounded in all the right places. She wore knee-length mukluks over skin-tight jeans and ran the distance with the grace of an animal, dodging puddles in her dash for the door. I had to find out all she knew about me, but that would have to wait. I had some research of my own to do. There was a suitcase lying open near the foot of the bed and a duffel bag next to it. Clothes, presumably mine, were hanging over a chair near the fire. I began by going through the pockets. What I found came in handy at a rather bizarre inquest next day.

"State your name, please, and spell it for the deputy," said the sheriff.

"Peter J. McCauley, I think." I began to spell it, but the sheriff waved his hand to shut me up.

"You'll have to do better than that. You can't say 'I think.' This is an official inquiry to determine the facts surrounding a man's death. Now let's start over again. And speak slowly so the deputy can get it all down proper. He ain't no fancy secretary and I have a hard enough time as it is deciphering his scrawl."

Our surroundings were weird, to say the least. The hunting lodge had once been a church and the sheriff and his deputy were seated at a plain wooden table on a raised platform. On the front wall was a large wooden cross and hanging on the cross was a moose head, a moth-eaten trophy

4

from some long-ago hunt. There were other trophies around the room – caribou, elk, even a stuffed grizzly standing on its hind legs and looking very menacing. In between were little plaques with religious sayings and a picture meant to represent Jesus with a holy light shining from His placid face. The witnesses – Robert Campbell, his wife Mary and I – sat in folding chairs at the foot of the raised platform. Behind us at the far end of the long room was a stone fireplace and clustered around it were several green felt gaming tables with built-in holders for beer cans. Along one wall were boxes of hunting gear, canned food and ammunition, and racks for packhorses. There were only a few small windows in the room and light from the fireplace cast eerie shadows on the sheriff's face that made him look more formidable than he probably was. He seemed like a reasonable man, if a somewhat suspicious one. I started over again, speaking slowly for the deputy.

"Sheriff, I got thumped pretty hard and to be honest I can't remember a thing. But I've had a chance to consider my predicament and I'll tell you everything I can about myself. But I can't swear to anything, because I just don't know anything for certain. I'll try to explain as I go along, okay?"

"That's fair enough. Now, get this down, Orville, and then, Mr. McCauley, you can fire away."

Orville chuckled nervously, but I didn't see the humor in it. There was a good chance I might face charges in the death of some guy named Frank Carter, and that was no laughing matter. I spoke slowly, deliberately.

"My name is Peter J. McCauley and I live at 110 Calhoun Terrace in San Francisco, California. I was born on June 16, 1933. I weigh 175 pounds, and once had brown hair, although it's gray now. My driver's license expires on my birthday in 1985. That information comes from a driver's license that I can only presume is mine. Other documents I found in my room indicate that I arrived in Anchorage on September 6, 1984, on a direct flight from SFO to

5

Anchorage International. I seem to have rented a Jeep C-J at the airport and drove here for a hunting expedition that somehow went terribly wrong. I got thumped by a slug big enough to kill a grizzly and I'm told the guy with me got zapped."

The deputy hesitated and looked to the sheriff for guidance.

"Put it down just that way, Orville, and we'll ask Mr. McCauley to define his terms."

"Thumped means I got hit, but I'm still here. Zapped means the other guy also got hit, but he's no longer here."

"What can you tell us about the deceased, Mr. McCauley? We identified him from his personal effects as Frank M. Carter. Does that name mean anything to you? Was he a friend of yours?"

"I don't honestly know."

"Did you travel here together?"

"I don't know."

"This is a very serious matter, Mr. McCauley. As the sheriff-coroner I've got a dead body on my hands and a lot of explaining to do. And you're not helping me very much."

"I'm doing the best I can. I'm as anxious as you are to get to the bottom of this."

"Yes, I'll bet you are. Tell you what, Mr. McCauley, Mrs. Campbell here can fill in a few gaps for us, so why don't we move along to her statement?"

Mary Campbell was very straightforward in her testimony. I'd arrived at the lodge along with the deceased and we appeared to be friends, although not particularly close friends. Our travel arrangements had been booked through a San Francisco agency, including a separate cabin for each of us here at Campbell Lodge. We'd been offered a double unit when we arrived, but turned it down, she said. The sheriff looked at me quizzically.

"I don't know," I shrugged. "Maybe Carter snored."

Mary went on to explain that we'd all been holed up for several days due to heavy rain here and blizzard conditions at the higher elevations and that we passed our time playing poker and that tempers grew short as the weather dragged on.

"Was there a fight?" asked the sheriff.

"No," she said. "They just seemed impatient with the rain and all, eager to get going. They were pretty cool to one another, and irritable. You know how it can get."

The sheriff nodded and Mary went on with her story, up to the moment she heard shots.

"You didn't witness the shooting?" the sheriff asked.

"No. I'd gone back toward the trailhead for a telescopic lens."

"And your husband?"

"He had remained with the truck."

"I notice," the sheriff said, "that all four of your weapons had been fired. Can you explain that?"

"We zeroed them in after breakfast before we drove up to the trailhead."

"All four of you?"

"You never know when you might get a shot," Mary explained.

"Was Mr. McCauley a good shot?"

"Yes, he was a very good shot. Both men were obviously familiar with weapons – good tight patterns in both targets."

The sheriff asked Robert Campbell if he had anything to add to his wife's statement, and he didn't. Campbell was an odd sort, a mean looking devil who'd be right at the top of my suspect list, if I were investigating this shooting. He was a big man, about six-feet-four, with a face that would make a baby cry, a scarred face that looked like an ice rink after a hockey game. He had narrow, hard eyes that looked holes through you. The sheriff handled him with kid gloves as if it were taken for granted that Campbell didn't have anything to do with this matter. That made me even more suspicious. The session lasted a little over an hour and it was clear the sheriff wasn't buying my amnesia story.

7

"Everything points to you as the one who shot Carter, McCauley, and yet I don't have enough hard evidence to hold you on criminal charges. It could be nothing more than a hunting accident and Lord knows we have enough of them around here. But I also want you to understand that this case isn't closed – far from it. My report will go to the district attorney and I'm sure his office will want to investigate it further. Therefore it's my duty to inform you that you must make yourself available to legal investigators of the State of Alaska whenever and wherever they choose to pursue the issue, understand?"

"Yes. Will I have to post bail?"

"No. You're not under arrest. You're free to go whenever the doctor says it's okay for you to travel. But we'll want to know where we can reach you."

The doctor wasn't due again until the following day, and it took two more days for the sheriff's office to get our statements typed and returned for us to sign. I took it very easy in the meantime, going over everything in my wallet and suitcase and duffel bag, time and time again. I could find nothing to indicate any family ties. The identification card in my wallet listed a Dr. David Ross at Letterman Hospital, Presidio of San Francisco, as the person to notify in case of an emergency. And among my toilet articles was a bottle of pills with a blank label issued by the government pharmacy at Letterman. I had no idea what they were and wasn't about to try them. An Army ID card in my wallet said I was Major Peter J. McCauley, retired. I had a bunch of scars that suggested I hadn't spent my military career behind a desk. There was a pattern of them running up my left leg, in my left side and my left forearm. It was obvious I'd been pretty badly shot up somewhere along the line. I wondered if that might be the key to all this.

I thought of putting a call though to Doctor Ross, but figured there really was no hurry. It was not at all bad recuperating at Campbell Lodge. The food was great and I was alone with a beautiful redhead. Her husband, Mary explained, had gone stateside on business and had instructed her to take care of me until I was fit to travel. She took very good care of me. She wrote down all the doctor's instructions, checked my bandage every day and fed\ me well from their freezer full of fish and game. The rains were over, the skies were clear and the air was cool and invigorating. We took long walks together through the valley with snow-covered, travel-poster peaks looming above us. We took our meals together and spent long hours talking. She told me the story of her life.

She said she'd been born there at the lodge and that her mother had died when she was very young. Her father had brought her up like a boy, taught her to hunt and fish. She was an expert tracker and knew how to take care of herself in the wilderness. And it was wild here, although only a few miles off State Highway 3, the main drag between Anchorage and Fairbanks. The two ran the lodge together and until her father died, leaving her the lodge, the cabins and stables, some packhorses and a tremendous tax bill. Then Robert Campbell showed up with a remarkable tale. He claimed to be her stepbrother by adoption, so to speak. He claimed that early in his life her father had married a young widow and adopted him, her infant son. Later the couple split and Mary's father trekked to Alaska to heal a broken heart. Eventually he took a second wife, had a daughter and went into the guide business. Mary said she doubted Campbell's story at first, but that he showed her a marriage certificate and adoption papers from White Pine County, Nevada, that seemed to prove his case. And because she needed a man around the place, she saw no reason to linger over any suspicions she might have. The guide business wasn't all that lucrative, there was that bill from the IRS, and Bob brought along some creative ideas on how to solve her financial problems. Somewhere along the line he had been ordained as a fundamentalist preacher, so he converted the lodge into a church for Sunday services and occasional prayer meetings. That brought some immediate tax relief. He also pointed out that since there was no blood relationship between them, there were certain advantages to filing a joint tax return. He was half again her age and not the kind of man she'd have chosen for a husband, had there been any others to choose from in that isolated place. But his proposal did make good business sense.

Over the past few years the Campbells managed to pay off the taxman and even show a modest profit. But Bob still had obligations to a congregation he served in California that demanded his attention, so he was away a lot and left Mary alone for months at a time to run the lodge. She was very competent. She did the bookkeeping, the cleaning and the cooking, and she was chief guide and outdoors expert. It was easy for me to imagine her in the latter roles after watching her tending the horses, splitting wood and cleaning the stables. The only thing that seemed incongruous was her skin. She had a pale, milky-white complexion. Her cheeks turned rosy in the cold, but she never seemed to tan or dry out or wrinkle, despite her outdoor life. She was beautiful, and I had a growing impulse to tell her so.

After a week the doctor dropped by again, took out the stitches in my scalp, put on a large adhesive bandage and pronounced me fit to travel. Mary was out in the stables when I told her, reluctantly, that the time had come for me to move on.

"I can imagine you're eager to get back to San Francisco."

"I do have a lot of questions that need answering."

"It's pretty late in the day to drive down…"

"I'll leave first thing in the morning."

We walked down the road to the entrance, shut the gate and hung up the closed sign. Later Mary broiled steaks and we had a quiet dinner there in that cavernous hall with the fire blazing in the hearth and that moose staring down from the cross. She even got out candles for the table. It was obvious she enjoyed polite company and got precious little of it from the rough and tumble hunters and fishermen that were her usual guests in this wild country. When we were through she came back to the cabin with me and we built a good fire to take the chill off the room. She helped me pack my things, then poked the fire and threw another log on while I sat on the edge of the bed watching her. When she'd finished she came over to me, flicking off the light on the way. She was beautiful in the firelight as she stood there with her hands on my shoulders.

"I'm going to miss you, Pete."

"It's been great, Red. I don't know how to thank you."

She was looking down at me, not listening to what I was saying, but unbuttoning her flannel shirt. She had trouble with the lower buttons, so I loosened her belt and her jeans. The shirt fell away easily then and she grasped my head gently and pressed my face against her naked breasts, tilting her head back and savoring the sensation of flesh against flesh. She was a hungry lover, eager and insatiable, almost animal-like in the vigor of her passion. She made love as if it would be the last time for a long time, storing up sensations as if the remembrance of them would keep her warm during the long, cold winter months. It was dark when I awakened amid a jumble of quilts and there was a chill in the room. I got up carefully so as not to disturb her and put more wood on the embers of our fire, kneeling there naked on the bearskin in front of the flames as they flickered to life. Suddenly I could feel her eyes on me and turned to see her up on one elbow, her gorgeous red hair all mussed and those clear, blue eyes staring at me with a voraciousness that was palpable.

"I fell asleep and let the fire go out," I said. "I guess I'm not as young as I used to be."

She didn't say a word, but got up slowly, never taking her eyes off mine, and strode across the room on those long, lovely legs and gently pressed me down on the bearskin rug in front of the fire and made me feel very, very young and vigorous again.

Chapter 2

The redhead wasn't the clinging type. She made coffee and warmed a couple of sweet rolls and we had breakfast there in the kitchen of the lodge, neither of us saying much. When it was time to go I apologized for all the trouble I'd been and thanked her for everything she'd done.

"No need to apologize," she said. "And you don't owe me any thanks. The pleasure was all mine."

There was the ring of sincerity in that last remark that for a moment made me want to chuck it all and stay right there, start life over again and forget about dredging up the past, whatever the past might have been. But the desire to know, to lay to rest whatever demons might lurk in the dark corners of my mind, was strong. I had to go, and she knew it. And of course there was her husband.

"Will I see you again?" she asked.

"If I don't discover I've got a wife and five kids, you probably will."

She smiled, leaned in through the Jeep's window and kissed me, a fleeting little peck.

"You could always bring them along," she said. "They might like it up here."

"So long, Red."

I kicked over the engine and got out of there and onto the highway before I changed my mind. I arrived at Anchorage International just before noon, turned in the Jeep and went to the ticket counter to get space on the next flight to San Francisco. To my surprise I learned there'd be no flight, not to San Francisco anyway.

"We made the changes you requested by phone, Mr. McCauley. But you're cutting it a bit close. You'll have to catch a charter to Skagway if you're going to get aboard the Stardancer. It sails at 4 p.m. tomorrow. Here are your tickets, including your connecting flight from Vancouver to SFO. Your best bet would be to get a flight out of Merrill Field. You might try AirAlaska. They make unscheduled hops to Skagway and may have something going out today. But you'd better hurry."

This was a surprise I didn't need. If I really had requested reservations for a cruise through the inland passage, why did I do it? And why tickets for one? Where did Frank Carter fit in? We supposedly were traveling together. Could it be that I actually planned to kill him and return alone? Or did he plan to kill me and travel back under my name? Or was someone else pulling the strings? I had no idea what lay at the end of this strange trip, but if I were going to get to the end of it, I'd have to follow the directions laid out for me. Who knows? Somewhere along the way I might find some answers.

Merrill Field handled private aircraft, executive planes and small commercial craft for sportsmen and tourists. The flyers were the heirs to the tradition of Alaska's famous bush pilots. I found AirAlaska out on the tarmac in the person of Mike Hobbs and his twin-engine Cessna. He said he'd be happy to fly me to Skagway just as soon as he finished his tune-up. "Cash on the barrel head."

"Will you settle for plastic? I'm low on cash."

"Sure, after you buy me lunch. Then I'll know your card is good."

We ate at the coffee shop in the terminal. Then I paid the tab and got a handful of twenties to tide me over. We took off into clear skies and headed out over the mountains, the inlets and the ice fields, with Mike offering a running spiel in his best tourist guide manner. In between his commentaries he revealed that he was a former Marine who'd served as a grunt in Vietnam, then got a transfer to the Naval Air Cadet program, where they decided he wasn't officer material, whatever that meant. But he did have a knack for flying, so they made him a warrant officer and sent him back to 'Nam to pilot a spotter plane for the big

13

gunboats lying off the coast, as well as for Marine mortar and artillery batteries. He'd come through without a scratch despite some pretty heavy action. I don't know if it was his war stories that jogged something deep in my muddled mind or what it was, but I had another flashback as we were flying over a patch of forestland. He's seen a moose in a swampy clearing and swooped in for a closer look. It was a steep dive and it sent blood rushing to my head. I got so dizzy I thought I was going to pass out. Then it happened. A scene flashed through my mind, just as real as the sound of bugles and shouting and gunfire that I heard as I lay there in the snow with a fresh head wound. It wasn't a moose that I saw bounding into the woods, it was a guy in a pointy hat and black pajamas and he was carrying an AK47 as he ran for cover. I heard the deafening clatter of automatic weapons erupting from a haze of blue smoke in the clearing.

"Pull up! Pull up, for Christ's sake?" I hollered.

"Hey, take it easy, man," said Hobbs as he eased out of the dive. "There's nothing to worry about. I got a handle on it, okay?"

"Sorry, Mike. I lost it. I don't know why. I guess I'm just not much of a flier." The poor guy was shaken by my sudden outburst and it put a damper on his travelogue, so we flew the rest of the way to Skagway in silence. We caught sight of the town just at sunset and Mike plugged into the tower's net to get landing instructions. It was nearly dark when we touched down. He was a bit cool as we parted company, but I thanked him for a smooth flight and grabbed a beat-up old cab for the nearest motel, which turned out to be right on the edge of the runway only a few blocks away. It was called the Gold Rush Lodge and it was newly refurbished and comfortable enough to suit me for the night.

Since it was still early I had time to kick back and reflect on what was turning out to be a puzzling string of events. There was damn little to go on, and each time I gathered up the facts and tossed them into the air they came down in a different pattern, not one of which made any sense

14

to me. I figured a guy could get paranoid trying to read too much into it, so I kept it as simple as possible: I was a retired Army officer on a hunting trip to Alaska. I took off with a buddy and somewhere up in the snow we parted company, only he did it the hard way by getting his head blown off. It may have been a tragic accident, as the sheriff suggested, but I'd gotten winged, too. Could it be...no, I refused to speculate. But who could blame me for being a little jumpy. It was dark and there seemed to be an unusual amount of traffic in the motel parking lot. I got nervous listening to tires crunching over the gravel, wondering who it was and if maybe someone out there was looking for me. It was tiresome, peeking through the drapes every few minutes, so I left my room, asked at the desk for the nearest restaurant and hiked a few blocks down to Broadway, the town's main drag, heading for a place called Irene's. I found myself looking nervously over my shoulder as I hurried through the darkness.

Irene's was a cozy little eatery on the upper edge of the business district, a comfortable, unpretentious place in a building that dated from the Gold Rush days, as did most of the structures along Broadway. Its menu was continental, but its special of the day was salmon with cucumber sauce and it sounded great. My waitress, a fresh-faced young mother who turned out to be a teacher in a summer job, took my order and carried it to the kitchen while I leaned back and soaked up the quiet. It was after eight o'clock and only two other tables were occupied. The atmosphere put me in a mellow mood and I felt a strange stirring, as if memories were supposed to flow through the empty chambers in my brain. But nothing came, except the waitress.

"Anything to drink?" she asked as she put down my salad.

"Got a wine list?"

She reached across the table for a little plastic stand with a few selections written in long hand – Chablis, Burgundy, White Zinfandel.

15

"House wines," I noted. "Is that all you've got?"

"On the back," she said. There I found a list of a dozen or so domestics.

"That Mondavi Fume Blanc," I asked, "is it Robert or C.K. Mondavi?"

"Robert," she said. "It's a California wine, I think."

Better than that, it was a Napa Valley wine, one of the very best, I thought as a bell rang somewhere in my mind.

"That's the secret word," I said. "Bring me a bottle, lightly chilled."

Its appearance was like old times, although I couldn't put my finger on them. The green bottle with the tasteful white label was instantly familiar. I could savor its clean, crisp taste even before she got the cork out of the bottle and splashed an ounce into my glass. It was perfect. And so was the salmon with cucumber sauce. Only the sourdough bread fell short of expectations. I mentioned it in response to the obligatory, "Is everything all right?"

"Everything except the bread," I answered. "I thought you folks up here invented sourdough, but this can't compare to San Francisco."

"We hear that all the time," she said with a smile, "usually from San Franciscans."

"Guilty," I confessed. "But the salmon was extraordinary. Fish lovers should beat a path to your door."

"Not likely this season," she said sadly. "The last cruise ship sails tomorrow. On Monday it's back to the schoolroom for me."

"And the long, cold winter," I observed.

"About eight months of it. I'll miss talking to people from the outside. The summer season is a big part of our lives here in Skagway."

There was a rumbling in the street and she looked up wistfully to listen.

"What is it?" I asked.

"Tour buses, campers, trailers, RVs – they've been pouring into town all day. The Stardancer docks in the

16

morning and sails in the afternoon with most of them aboard. She'll be carrying away the life's blood of this community."

"There's always next season," I said. "I'll try to send a few more San Franciscans your way. That was a great dinner." I included a generous tip on my bill in an effort to bolster her spirits.

Broadway was alive with a throng of tourists wending their way in and out of shops, bags laden with gifts and mementos to take stateside. I marveled at the way a determined citizenry had turned a veritable ghost town from 1898 into a modern tourist boomtown with renovated Nineteenth Century buildings flourishing as hotels, shops and restaurants that managed to capture the aura of a bawdy and colorful past. The past held a particular fascination for me, since the drive to recapture my own was quickly becoming an obsession. It had been a productive evening. I had recalled things tonight that only yesterday were not in my memory. And if I could recall anything, no matter how trivial, maybe someday I could recall everything. I walked back to the motel clinging to that hope. But in the emptiness of my room I realized that it was one thing to remember a Napa Valley wine and San Francisco sourdough bread; it was quite another to rebuild a life that might be best forgotten. It had been a long day since I'd said goodbye to Mary Campbell, and I fell asleep with thoughts of her rather than worries about my past.

Chapter 3

The Stardancer lay with her cargo hold open, her freight gangway resting on the landing like a huge tongue, lapping up all manner of recreational vehicles and swallowing them into her hold for the journey through the inland passage. I caught a horse-drawn jitney outside the motel and the driver, a chatty young woman who spent the off-season driving a snowplow for the highway department, let me out near the foot of the wharf where members of the purser's staff were checking in luggage for boarding passengers. They looked over my tickets, tagged my bags and directed me to the passenger gangway that led to the main deck. I gave the pony's nose a rub for luck, slipped the jitney driver a twenty for her trouble and went aboard. An assistant purser took my ticket and checked the charts spread before her on her table.

"Oh, good, Mr. McCauley. We're happy to have you aboard. I've got good news for you. We've been able to upgrade you to a starboard cabin on the Club Deck at no extra cost. We've had a few cancellations. Let me see, you want second seating, right?"

She didn't really expect an answer. She was one of those efficient types who chatted amiably to put you at ease, but was more interested in her work than in you. She wore a navy blue suit and a simple white blouse. Her nametag told me she was Cynthia, Asst. Purser. She ran her finger over the dining room seating chart and found my place.

"Here you are. You'll complete table one-sixteen. Breakfast at eight forty-five, lunch at one-thirty, dinner at eight-thirty."

She scribbled it on a form and handed it to me, looking at me for the first time and noticing the bandage on my forehead and my bruises, the remnants of two black eyes.

"Oh, my! We have a doctor on board, Mr. McCauley, if you should need one. I hope you're feeling all right." By the time she finished speaking she was already back to writing on her chart.

"It's nothing serious," I said. "I fell out of an airplane."

"Well, we hope you'll enjoy your voyage," she said, apparently not having heard a word I said. She was looking beyond me to the next passenger in line. The form she handed me listed my cabin number and advised me that it would be available at four o'clock and that in the meantime all the lounges were open for my convenience. I went directly to the Club Deck anyway on the chance that my cabin might be made up. It was locked, but down the passageway a pair of stewards pushed a luggage cart in my direction, dropping off bags at cabins as they passed. I recognized my things in their load.

"How are chances of getting in?" I asked as they arrived at my door.

"Four o'clock," said one of the stewards. "Cabin's not ready yet."

It was a stock answer. He obviously didn't know whether my cabin was made up or not, since he hadn't yet opened the door. The other steward slipped a passkey – a plastic card – into the slot and pushed his way in with my suitcase and duffel bag. I could see over his shoulder that the beds were made up and everything seemed to be in order. The first steward was on his way down the passageway with his cart when the second steward came out of my cabin. He smiled and closed the door without latching it.

"Four o'clock," he said with a wink and a nod. I let myself in and closed the door behind me. It was a small cabin with two beds, a table between the headboards and a large porthole that looked out over the inlet to the ferry landing across the way. It was cold outside and a stiff wind was raising whitecaps on the water. The skies were leaden and there was nothing to lure me out on deck, so I stretched out on the bed and in no time at all managed to doze off. I slept for more than an hour until my room steward let himself in carrying a basket of fruit and a handful of promotional literature, instructions and a map of each deck. He was startled to see me.

"So sorry," he said. "I didn't know the cabin was occupied."

He was an elderly Filipino and was falling all over himself in embarrassment.

"Forget it," I said. "I let myself in early to get some rest. You understand."

"Sure, sure. You have all your luggage? Anything I can get for you? My name's Ferdy. I'm your steward. I take care of everything. You just call me – here on this phone. I'll get whatever you want. You want lunch? I get you lunch. You want a snack, I get…"

"No, no thanks, Ferdy. I just want to rest before dinner. Thanks anyway."

He was no kid, about sixty, I guessed, and seemed genuinely anxious to please. Maybe it was his way of nailing down a generous end-of-the-voyage gratuity. His nametag said he was Ferdinand, but if he preferred Ferdy, then Ferdy it would be. After he was gone I unpacked my bags and stretched out on the bed again to look through the brochures and the information kit. Before long I'd read everything there was to read and I was getting bored. The engines were throbbing but we weren't under way yet. I called room service and ordered a martini – straight up, very dry and hold the olive. Ferdy was there with it by the time I was out of the shower. The cocktail glass was nicely frosted and beside it was a shot glass with two huge olives skewered on a swizzle stick.

"Thanks, Ferdy, and keep the change. By the way, I asked them to hold the olives."

"On the side," he explained with a big smile. "In case you change your mind. No trouble. Ferdy take them back."

He pocketed the bill I'd handed him, picked up the tray and went out the door, popping the olives into his mouth as he went. They hadn't been for me at all. They were for wily old Ferdy. I dressed for dinner and went out on deck. The crew was casting off the mooring lines and I watched for a few minutes. The wind was up and it looked as if rain wasn't far off, but I stayed on deck to watch the ship pull away, leaving Skagway in a pall of mist and low clouds that already obscured the mountains that locked the town into its tight little cove. Then I went aft to the Sundown Lounge for another martini, this one without olives.

I didn't see her when she came in. She'd apparently been talking to a group of passengers seated by the windows looking out at the rough sea as we headed down the Lynn Canal en route to Haines. I couldn't miss her as she approached. She was medium height, blonde hair – not natural – and well tanned. There was a trim body inside that neat little uniform and though her makeup was a little heavy, it seemed to look just right on her. She walked confidently through the lounge, very much aware of the heads she turned, but obviously comfortable with the attention.

"Well, Mr. McCauley, I see you haven't fallen overboard."

That caught me off guard.

"So, you were listening after all."

"It was my very busiest time. I didn't mean to be rude."

"You weren't. You were professional, efficient. But when I can't make eye contact I get to feeling like a piece of furniture. Sorry if I…"

"Nothing to be sorry about, Mr. McCauley. I've got time for a little eye contact now, if you like."

"Then let me buy you a drink."

"That I can't do. I'm still on duty. We're taking aboard passengers at Haines."

"Okay, then, just a little eye contact and conversation. How come I got upgraded?"

"It's late in the season. We're running below capacity. The weather's turning cold and travelers are turning to

21

warmer climates. If we can foster a little good will by upgrading some of our passengers, why not?"

"It makes sense. And what do you do during the off season, go into dry dock?"

"No, we cruise to Mexico during the winter months – Baja, Cabo San Lucas, Mazatlan, Puerto Vallarta. You ought to try it. Have you sailed much?"

"Not at all, unless you count troopships. But I may take it up. I like the service, the drinks, the eye contact."

"We pride ourselves on our service, Mr. McCauley. You keep away from the rail now, ya' hear?"

There weren't many men in the room, but every one of them followed her with his eyes as she left and I was no exception. I got another drink and took it over to a seat by the windows to watch the rain sweep down the decks. It was nearly dark and pouring when we arrived at Haines. The waiter brought me a dish of peanuts and I settled in for the storm, managing to keep warm despite the martinis, which were bitter cold and powder dry. It was dark when second call came for dinner. The dining room was two decks below and the sea was rough, but I made it down the stairs by keeping a tight grip on my martini glass. Little old ladies, and there were lots of them on this cruise, didn't seem to have as much trouble navigating as I did. I guess it would take awhile to get my sea legs.

With just a little guidance from the wait staff I located table one-sixteen which was occupied by five little old ladies who greeted me with friendly nods. At the window, sitting across from one another, was a couple who stared into the darkness seemingly ignoring the LOLs. I put down my martini glass at the empty space and introduced myself.

"Hi," I said. "My name's Pete McCauley and I guess I'll be joining you."

The ladies were suddenly atwitter, then shyly offered their names, all at once, until a spokeswoman took over and performed more orderly introductions. I nodded to each, smiling pleasantly, while noting that the couple at the window was studiously ignoring me.

"Hi!" I repeated for their benefit. "I'm Pete McCauley."

The woman looked at me as if I had my elbow in my salad, which I didn't, and her husband gave me a fleeting glance and mumbled "Felkerson" while reaching for a basket of rolls. The ladies nodded knowingly, each wearing her best "I-told-you-so" expression. The LOL across the table informed me that she and her colleagues were members of an Altar Guild from Walla Walla and that they had lost a colleague to heart palpitations shortly before sailing and had put her aboard a plane for Anchorage and a flight home. It was her seat that I now occupied. That automatically made me a part of their camp, and that made the Felkersons the enemy. If I were to be an LOL recruit, I had to undergo some basic training. First of all, I learned to keep my hands off the food until after grace had been offered. The Felkersons, of course, were munching on their rolls. I also learned that the Felkersons had boarded at Skagway and immediately squatted in the window seats that previously belonged to the LOLs. Hence the chilly atmosphere. At the moment, however, it was time for grace.

"I believe it's your turn, Samantha," said the spokeswoman. Samantha immediately launched into the longest prayer I'd ever heard, laced with all sorts of thees and thous and delivered with such fervor I was convinced I wasn't going to hang around for *my* turn. I didn't know anything about theology, but I was sure mealtime wasn't going to be any fun if I had to be that grateful for tournedos of beef en brochette. And as for wine with dinner, forget it. Henceforth dinner for me was going to be a steak sandwich at the Lido Bar and Grill on the sun deck, with a martini or two before, wine during and a Drambuie after.

I spent a restless first night aboard ship. Maybe it was the vibrations that the engine sent through the vessel, or maybe the rough sea and the slight pitch and roll. All sorts of crazy things went through my head, but the imagination can run wild when there's nothing on your mind to impede it. To keep from worrying about all the strange noises and movements I tried to focus on Cynthia, the assistant purser with the nice tan. Warm thoughts of her took my mind off drowning in an icy fjord and it sure beat counting sheep. I was dead to the world when the squawk box in my cabin chimed to announce the first seating for breakfast. I got up and showered away the cobwebs. I had no appetite, but there was plenty of time to work one up before the second seating. There were jogging clothes in my duffel bag and a track on the topmost deck. It was a lucky decision. I found Cynthia at one of the exercise stations, stretching those long, tan legs of hers and working up a sweat that matted the hair under her headband.

"I'm glad I ran into you," I said. "I've got a complaint."

"Good morning, Mr. McCauley. Don't tell me you fell out of bed."

She was never going to let me forget that airplane gag. I explained that my table companions weren't exactly my type and wondered if she could change my seating assignment. For instance, I thought it might be great to dine with her tonight.

"And risk the wrath of the Altar Guild ladies from Walla Walla! No way! They've already asked me to give the boot to the Felkersons so they can reclaim the window seats. I had to turn them down, too."

"But do I have to be their consolation prize?"

She ignored the question, puffed through her fiftieth deep knee bend, then leaned forward at the waist and grasped the horizontal bar with both hands, stretching her shoulders and back. The position was provocative, with her derriere poked up in the air that way, and she caught me admiring her form.

"Why don't you try this?" she asked peering up at me from under her arm. "It takes the kinks out of your back and makes you feel ten feet tall."

"I already feel ten feet tall. Why are you dodging my request, is it out of order?"

"It's very flattering, really, but I have to think of the others at your table. You wouldn't want to hurt their feelings, would you?"

"They won't miss me. We had dinner together, nothing more. I don't think any heavy relationships are likely to come of it."

"Give it a chance, Mr. McCauley. You never know what might develop."

"I could say the same to you. Give me a chance. You never know what might develop."

"I'm only interested in developing muscles right now, Mr. McCauley. How about a turn around the track?"

"Fine, for starters. But my name is Pete. Can't I be Pete while you're off duty?"

"Why not?" she said with a smile that could have melted the glacier we were gliding past. We spent half an hour jogging in the crisp morning air as the vessel churned down Tracy Arm. By the time the sun had taken the chill off the day we'd finished a snack of fruit and coffee at the Lido. She was fun to talk to, one of those women who can make a guy think he's really something special, smiling all the time, laughing at just the right places. And the eye contact – the eye contact made me think of warm summer nights on the Marina Green or sailing on San Francisco Bay with the spindrift cool on my face. Then she had to leave to get ready for work. And I still hadn't gotten a commitment from her, even for dinner. But I was looking forward to jogging next morning. I could get myself into truly remarkable shape with her as a pacer.

I had another cup of coffee after she left. I was seated facing the stern of the ship and just ahead of me was the Jacuzzi with its hot, roiling water giving off clouds of steam. A young family was about to enter the pool. He was Caucasian, she a willowy Eurasian, and their son a handsome lad of about eight who seemed to combine his parents' best features. They slipped out of their robes and eased themselves into the water. It was as simple as that, a perfectly natural and innocent scene, but it sent a blinding flash through my head. The blood throbbed in my temples, my vision became blurred and I was sure I was going to pass out. I knocked my coffee over as I staggered to my feet, grasping my head. A waiter rushed to grab me.

"Are you all right, sir?"

I looked at him through a gray haze, held on to his shoulders with both hands and hung on for dear life. A woman at a nearby table let out a little scream, loud enough to shock me into sharper awareness. I made a quick apology to the waiter, mumbling something about my head injury and got out of there as quickly as I could. Something was trying to work its way into my consciousness, I was sure of it. And it wasn't recollections of warm nights on the Marina Green or sailing on San Francisco Bay. It was something much more ominous. But whatever it was, it never became clear. I went back to my cabin to lie down, thinking that maybe if I could just relax and let my mind go blank some figment of my past might return to give me a clue. But every time I wiped the slate clean, Cynthia appeared there. I either had to give thoughts of her free rein or try to forget her altogether. And I already had forgotten far too much of my life.

Chapter 4

Her name was Cynthia Albright, an Indiana girl who had always wanted to be a nurse but decided to be an airline stewardess when, after two years of college, the money ran out and she grew impatient to be on her own. That was when she was young and impressionable. That was before she grew tired of parrying the advances of inebriated businessmen, before she'd been bedded by a fast-talking pilot, before she had fallen in love with an idealistic young law student, and before she had married him and then lost him forever in some God-forsaken rice paddy in Vietnam. It was then she pulled back from the world for a while, collected herself and ventured forth again, this time more savvy, more guarded, more certain of what she wanted out of life – and what she didn't want. One thing she didn't want was the nomadic life of a flight attendant, although she still loved to travel and meet new people. The steamship industry offered a comfortable compromise. Men, for the most part, didn't travel alone on cruise ships the way they did on jetliners. They traveled with their wives or lovers. I was the rare exception, fortunately, because she was ready for a little experimentation. Nothing serious – that was understood from the beginning. And it was to be on her terms. She was anything but a dumb blonde and she refused to be taken for one or treated like one. She knew her way around and she knew what she wanted, and for the moment – just for the moment – she wanted me, on her terms and with no strings attached.

She was very frank in telling me all this and I wanted to be frank with her, too. But how would it have sounded?

"I'm suffering from amnesia. I don't know who I am or what I'm doing here. I think I live in San Francisco and I'm on my way there now to see if anyone knows me and can tell

me how I got this way and why. Of course, I don't know what I'll find there. Maybe I'll find a wife and kids. Maybe I'll find I'm wanted for murder."

No, I couldn't tell her that and I didn't. I made up a story based on what little I did know, and hedged when it looked as if I might have to go too far beyond the obvious.

She suspected I was hiding something, I could tell by those deep brown eyes that searched my face when I spoke. But she could see I wore no wedding ring, nor any sign of one. That seemed to be enough. She could accept me on those terms, because in her heart she didn't believe she'd ever see me again. What she did learn about me she liked, and what I hid from her she didn't care about anyway. We were good company for one another. The cruise was brief and our time together aboard ship very limited. There could be no harm in a little self-indulgence. We couldn't have dinner together, but we did get together in the lounge for a drink at night and we enjoyed an hour together in our morning workout. To my surprise she agreed to come to my cabin that last night before the Stardancer arrived in Vancouver, with the understanding that she'd have to get up early and might be gone before I awakened. She took her bourbon with ice and just a splash of plain water. I called room service and Ferdy brought a tray with her drink and for me my usual martini in a carafe with stuffed olives on the side. Cindy – she insisted I call her that now that we were on more intimate terms – arrived in her smartly tailored uniform, carrying a large purse that served as her overnight bag. There was nothing coy about her. After a drink and some light conversation she excused herself and went into the bathroom to slip out of her uniform. She came out in a modest negligee and a warm smile.

"Your turn, Pete. Or would you like me to do it?"

"I can manage," I said.

"I'll turn down the bed."

When I came out I saw that she'd poured me another martini from the carafe. She'd put the olives in the glass, but

28

that didn't matter. I wasn't interested in another drink. I had other things on my mind and so did she. By the time I'd hung up my clothes she was in my arms and we weren't thinking about anything but each other. She was a very loving and passionate woman, deliberate, unhurried in everything she did, thorough, thoughtful, wonderful. She believed in stimulating all the senses, lights on, eyeball to eyeball. If it felt good, do it. If you wanted anything, just ask. She was beautiful, all over beautiful, with a firm body that belied her years, a lean and supple body. Our morning workouts were nothing compared to the one we enjoyed that night. And if eye contact enhanced conversation, it raised lovemaking to ecstatic levels. I would never forget those deep brown eyes and the way they rolled back in pure pleasure as we approached a climax. It was after midnight when she fell asleep in sweet exhaustion, her head on my shoulder, her hair spread across my chest. I reached up and turned out the lights and when the first call to breakfast chimed me awake, I realized she was gone, just as she said she'd be.

The ship was already docked when I hurried down for a cup of coffee. Passengers were all over the place, stacking their luggage in the passageways for pick up, hurrying to and from breakfast, bidding farewell to new friends, making soon-to-be-forgotten plans to meet again another day. I kept an eye open for Cindy, but didn't see her. I didn't want to look too hard; she wouldn't have wanted that. I just wanted one more glimpse of her, although it really wasn't necessary. I'd never forget our night together and that was more than any man could ever want. I finished my coffee, said goodbye to the LOLs of table one-sixteen and nodded to the Felkersons, who looked particularly dour. I wondered if they'd hold on to those window seats until the Walla Walla ladies disembarked.

Ferdy's work cart was in front of my cabin door when I returned and I noticed he'd already tidied up the room. The serving tray from last night was on his cart and I noticed the martini Cindy had poured for me was still there, untouched except for the olives. Ferdy, the old devil, had snatched the olives. I walked into the room, peeling off a couple of twenties to tip him for his service, but it wouldn't be necessary. Ferdy lay dead on the bathroom floor. Whatever got him got him fast. He hadn't quite made it to the commode before he vomited and died. His eyes were wide open and so was his mouth and I could see bits of green and red. He might have choked on the olives; more likely they were poisoned. I wasn't going to hang around to find out, not with one unexplained death already on my hands. My bags had been picked up, so there was only my toilet kit to grab before getting the hell out of there. A backwoods sheriff might let an amnesia victim off the hook temporarily, but the Vancouver cops would be harder to convince. There was no way I could have explained this one. I left the door open just enough so that no one walking by could see poor Ferdy, but anyone looking for him would have no trouble finding him. I got down to the dock as quickly as I could, located my baggage and hailed a cab for the airport.

I had time to think about it on the plane and it all came up bad. I was a marked man and had escaped by the skin of my teeth twice in as many weeks. And whoever was after me would go to any length to see me dead – from the wilderness of Alaska to a ship at sea. When the flight attendant came around taking orders for drinks, I declined. There might be someone in the galley intent of having a try at me. I stayed alert all the way to SFO, watching everyone who went up or down the aisle. In an effort to ameliorate my growing paranoia I focused my thoughts on Cindy and our wonderful night together. I wanted to get in touch with her again, and soon.

* * *

Everything about San Francisco was familiar, including the miserable ride into town from the airport during the rush hour. I felt I knew every landmark I passed, and yet where did I fit in? Things didn't get cloudy until I left the limousine

30

downtown and hailed a cab, asking to be taken to Calhoun Terrace.

"Gimme a clue, mate," said the driver.

Damn those cobwebs in my brain! To me Calhoun Terrace was just an address on a driver's license. I couldn't place it.

"Wait a minute," said the cabby. "Isn't that up on Telegraph Hill?"

"Yes. Telegraph Hill," I said as the curtains slowly parted. "Just below Montgomery off Union Street."

"Gotcha, mate."

I got off at the intersection so he wouldn't have to turn around in the little cul-de-sac by my apartment building. The view was immediately familiar as I strolled over the crest of the hill and looked out at the bay. Streams of vehicles, an unbroken string of taillights stretching across the Bay Bridge, vanished behind Yerba Buena Island, then reappeared and continued on toward the East Bay hills. If this could come back to me, everything else could, too, with a little help. I got out my keys and studied them. Yes, here was the key to the security gate. I'd used it a thousand times. And behind the gate was the stairway that led down to my apartment. Down, down they went – eighty-eight steps past all the other apartment units to the very bottom where my little hideaway hung precariously to the side of the sheer rock with nothing beneath it but a couple of spindly support pillars, before the drop to Sansone Street. I let myself in and looked around. Windows ran the length of the apartment, an unbroken wall of glass except where the fireplace and chimney interrupted the spectacular view. I knew this place, all right. How could I have forgotten it? But the strain was catching up to me. My head ached. A lot of things were coming back, crowding into my memory again. It was as if I'd been away for years and forgotten everything, and now everything was trying to come back at once. All but the most critical things, like who I really was and why anyone would want me dead. There was a pile of mail on the table near the door, including a government check, the familiar green computer card showing through the address window of the tan envelope; a telephone bill, magazines, the usual stuff that accumulates over a couple of weeks. Then she appeared.

"You forgot to knock," she said. "I heard you go by, but you forgot to knock."

She was standing in the doorway, just a kid, young enough to be my daughter. She was barefoot and dressed in jeans and a sloppy tie-died shirt. Her hair was pulled back in a ponytail and her face was open and innocent, even in a pout.

"Sorry, I guess I was preoccupied."

"You *always* knock."

"I'm exhausted. I just got off a plane. It's been a long day."

"You're all right, aren't you, Pete? Not having any problems?"

"What kind of problems? Don't I look all right?"

"You know very well what kind of problems. Have you been taking your pills?"

"No, I guess I haven't. How can you tell?"

"Because you're acting weird, that's how. You know what the doctor..."

She'd stepped closer to me and noticed the raw scar on my scalp.

"Jesus, Pete! How'd that happen?"

"It's a long story and I've got a helluva headache. Can we do this tomorrow, whatever it is we're doing?"

"Now I know you haven't been taking your pills. You get right in here."

She led me into the tiny kitchen, got a glass and a bottle of pills from the cupboard and ran the tap. The pills were in an unmarked bottle, just like the ones I'd found in my suitcase.

"You take this right away, doctor's orders," she said, sounding more than ever like a daughter scolding her old man. She handed me a pill and a glass of water. I'd had too many close calls lately to willingly take what might be my last gulp, so I palmed the pill and tossed back the water while she watched me with a frown on her pretty face.

"What was that," I asked, "aspirin?"

"You know it wasn't. Now come and lie down until you're feeling better."

She led me into the bedroom in the rear of the apartment and put my shoes in the closet while I stretched out on the bed. It all seemed very homey, but I had a sudden sense of foreboding. Who was she and what was in that pill she handed me? I knew I was expected to relax, so I pretended to doze off while she puttered around the bedroom, unpacking my bags and putting away my clothes. She seemed to know where everything went. I closed my eyes and tried again to focus on the events of the past few days, but nothing made any sense yet. This girl seemed to know a lot about me. She might be the key I needed to unlock those areas of my mind that were still closed to me. Next thing I knew she was bending over me, so close I could feel her breath on my face. She gave me a little peck on the cheek, then tiptoed out the door so as not to awaken me. In a moment I heard her snap an audio tape into the cassette player and the soothing strains of Beethoven's Sixth, the *Pastoral*, filled the apartment. I heard the front door close quietly and in seconds I heard footsteps overhead. Her apartment was just above mine. I got up in the gathering darkness and made a survey of my quarters. They were well furnished, definitely a bachelor's pad, albeit an eclectic one. The books on the shelves ranged from Montaigne to Camus, from Jefferson to Twain and Wylie and Salinger. The tapes were equally diverse, a little heavy on traditional jazz, but with a respectable collection of Beethoven and Mozart and a newly minted album of J.S. Bach. I noticed a Time magazine lying open on the arm of a recliner chair that faced out to the bay. The night was clear and the water glittered with reflected lights. I retreated to the bedroom with the mail and the magazine and pulled the drapes across the window. Then I turned on the bedside lamp

33

and searched the mail for clues. It wasn't much help. Bills, mostly, from which I learned that I charged far too many nights on the town. As if to balance these expenditures, there was the pension check made out to Major Peter J. McCauley, Ret. It was quite a respectable sum.

None of this told me much, but the magazine caused some stirrings. It was dated four weeks earlier and had a photograph of President Ronald Reagan on the cover. It was open to a report on the funeral of four-star Gen. Harrison J. Parks. He had quite a resume. He was called Hell-for-Leather Harry, last in his class at West Point, served as a battalion commander in the Phillipines and fled the islands in 1942 as a member of MacArthur's staff. He earned his first star on the beaches of Normandy and was a veteran of the bloody fighting in the frozen mountain passes around the Changjin reservoir in Korea, one of the top commanders of the landing at Inchon, and legendary chief of Ranger operations in Vietnam. After defying death during an illustrious thirty-year career, much of it in the thick of combat, Parks had retired some ten years ago and had died quietly in his bed in nearby Woodside of natural causes. I remembered Harry Parks. How could I have forgotten him? I could see myself now as a young platoon sergeant during the retreat down Korea's Nightmare Alley, holding a battered band infantrymen together after the death of our company commander. It was Hell-for-Leather Harry himself who commissioned me a second lieutenant one dark and frigid dawn and ordered me and my unit to fight a holding action while U.N. forces retreated toward Hungnam.

That was it! That was the night of the bombardment, the night of the blaring bugles that struck terror in the heart of every man in my command until the first wave of Chinese infantry reached our perimeter. Then the crackle of small arms fire and the clash of bayonets drove terror from our minds and fixed our attention on only one thing – survival. I doubt that General Parks expected any of us to come out of it alive, but some of us did and we got little bronze medals for

34

our effort. A few months later Parks had me assigned to his staff. That probably was how I got to Vietnam, although memories beyond Korea were still fuzzy. There was a photograph of the general accompanying his obituary and another of the graveside ceremony at Golden Gate National Cemetery. Accepting the neatly folded American Flag that had draped his casket was his daughter, Elizabeth Mahon, and her teenage son. A veil obscured her face; the boy's was hauntingly familiar.

Chapter 5

It was one of those bakery mornings when everything seemed to have been created fresh just a moment before dawn. The sky had never been so clear and blue, I thought as I lingered over my coffee, looking out over the pristine panorama of San Francisco Bay. The glistening water was flecked with white canvas as weekend sailors took to the sea. My nubile neighbor was up, too. I could hear her footsteps on the floor above. It wasn't long before she was at my door.

"Come in, it's unlocked."

She was wearing the same outfit she had worn the night before, but today she had on beach walks. She was a pretty little thing, with dark eyes and olive skin, black hair and high cheekbones. She was almost Eurasian in appearance, all but the eyes. The eyes were decidedly Occidental, wide and round and proud. Remembering our meeting the night before, I was curious about her parentage, wondering if I had any role in it.

"How are you feeling this morning?" she asked as she slipped into a chair and leaned close to study my face.

"I'm just fine. How do I look to you, Doc?"

She wrinkled her brow and shook her head.

"You're still not yourself. Did you take a pill yet?"

"No. I don't like taking pills, particularly when I don't know what they're for. I won't try to put you on. I had an accident, a hunting accident. A slug creased my skull and I can't remember a lot of things. I suspect that you know more about me than I do, so you're going to have to help me get my bearings. Let's start with the pills. What are they and why do I have to take them?"

She was immediately suspicious and on her guard. She reached out and gently ran a finger over the raw scar on my head. It seemed to satisfy her.

"Jesus, Pete, you could've been killed. We've got to get you to Doctor Ross. It's been a couple of weeks already – and you not taking your pills! That's probably why you seem different. You're supposed to take them regularly, you know."

"No, I don't know. Why do I take them? What's wrong with me?"

"They're to help you relax. You get pretty wound up sometimes. Don't you remember? You get these flashbacks to the war and all. The pills help keep you on an even keel. But to forget everything! Jeez, this could be serious. You could go off the deep end again. Do you even know who I am?" That suspicious look came over her again.

"Sure. You're my upstairs neighbor. You're pretty as a picture and you seem to take very good care of me. How's that?"

"Not good enough. Remember B.J. – Barbara Jean Franklin? You've forgotten ol' B.J.? You really know how to hurt a girl, you know that? I'd say something dumb, like you men are all alike, except I think you really have lost your mind."

"Memory," I corrected her. "And don't take it personally. I didn't even know my own name until I looked it up on my driver's license."

I told her about the hunting accident, but I didn't mention Frank Carter or the fact that he was dead. I also assured her that I hadn't suffered any ill effects from not taking the pills, although I suspected now that much more than a shotgun slug was to blame for my muddled memory. I was very selective about what I told B.J. about my trip home. The pills, or the lack of them, might well have something to do with my paranoia. The hunting "accident" and Ferdy's death would remain my secret for now. Being spooked by an imaginary assassin might be the result of withdrawal symptoms from the drug Doctor Ross was giving me.

"Now it's your turn," I said. "Tell me about yourself and see if you can ring my bells."

She smiled shyly as if she weren't used to talking about herself, embarrassed about revealing the details of her life. She said she was an Army brat whose parents were divorced. She'd lived in San Francisco most of her life, alone in the apartment upstairs for the past couple of years. She worked at the telephone company as a service rep and she met me at Letterman Hospital at The Presidio. We shared the same shrink.

"Doctor Ross," I said. "But what was your problem? Surely not post-combat stress syndrome."

She was more than embarrassed, she was in obvious pain as she rambled through her memories, most of them unpleasant. She was baring her soul to me and it wasn't easy. I was sorry I'd asked, but once she got started there was no stopping her.

"My father – well, he had an unhappy marriage. He and my mother fought all the time and I knew early on that somehow I was the cause of it. He usually got the worst of it and I always felt sorry for him. I grew up hating my mother, while Dad and I just grew closer. Too close, if you know what I mean. It started out innocently enough, but we got more and more involved, you know? Well, my mother caught us together a few years ago and really flipped out. You see, they'd been living apart for some time and I lived with her and was seeing Dad on the sly. She was about to bring criminal charges against him when I reminded her that I was eighteen then and an adult. I refused to cooperate with her. I loved my father and felt sorry for him and could never testify against him. And frankly I liked being with him, if you get my drift. I just have a thing about older men, I guess."

That was where Doctor Ross came into the picture. He was counseling them both, father and daughter. When her father was transferred out of the area, B.J. continued taking her problems to Ross' couch. He was trying to redirect her interest toward men her own age. Apparently it wasn't working.

"Oh, it helped some," she explained. "I don't blame myself now for breaking up their marriage. He said most kids feel that way when their parents split. He also helped me understand that my relationship with my father was abnormal. He says it was aimed at consoling my father and getting back at my mother for being mean to him. I don't know about that, but I know I still don't like men my own age. I don't think they're men at all. They're too – too aggressive, too clumsy, too selfish and weird. I could go on about it, but I can't believe there's anything wrong with me just because I don't like immature males."

It was becoming disturbingly clear why she had latched on to me, and the very thought of it made me nervous. She was only twenty-two and she was a very desirable young lady. I was afraid to get into the matter of our personal relationship, but it was obvious that we were more than neighbors. How much more remained to be seen, but at least it was legal. A guy can't be charged with incest just because he's a father figure. I had to get my mind off that track, so back to Doctor Ross.

"I think it's time to get in touch with your psychiatrist," I suggested.

"*Our* psychiatrist," she corrected me. "We can give him a call anytime. He'll be at the hospital today. He usually sees working guys on Saturday and he'll certainly see you. Rank has its privileges, you know. And if he's not in, I've got his private number."

It never occurred to her that I was suggesting *she* see Ross. She was convinced there was nothing wrong with her. But I had to see him anyway to find out about the pills and probably a lot of other things he could tell me. B.J. had an old beat up Bug she insisted on driving. She said my car wasn't in driving condition and hinted that I wasn't either. I might "flip out," as she put it. I had no such qualms, but let her have her way. We went straight out Union Street, over Russian Hill to Van Ness and then to Lombard Street to the

Presidio. B.J. waited for me in the parking lot while I went in to see Ross, who was more than anxious to see me.

"Yes," he began with a raised eyebrow. "I was surprised by Miss Franklin's call. She said you were off your pills and not yourself. Is that right?"

"I could use some help, Doc, but not the kind that comes from pills. Fact is I can't recall why I'm taking them. I suffered a head injury recently and I can't remember a lot of things – you, for instance. If you can tell me why I'm taking the damned things, maybe we can go on from there."

The nameplate on his desk said he was a colonel. He appeared to be in his sixties, well preserved the way many small, wiry guys seem to be. He was bald on top with neatly clipped patches of black hair over his ears and graying sideburns. He wore rimless glasses pushed far down on his nose and a sported a black moustache shaved to a thin line just above his lip. He was not in uniform, but wore casual clothes under a white medical jacket. The license on his wall said he'd graduated from the University of California Medical School here in San Francisco. On the desk in front of him was a fat folder that he toyed with as we talked. I took it to be my medical file.

"So you don't remember a thing, is that it?" he asked somewhat skeptically.

"Not exactly," I explained. "I remembered San Francisco, or a lot of it, but I'd forgotten B.J. and that would seem to take a lot of forgetting."

He didn't take kindly to that. If looks could kill, my interview would be over. He obviously didn't approve of my relationship with B.J., whatever it might be. I also got the idea that he didn't believe a word I was saying.

"Suppose you start from the beginning," he said. "Tell me just how it happened."

He projected an air of superiority that set me on edge. I didn't like him and I wasn't going to tell him any more than I'd told B.J. He looked like the type who'd turn me over to the cops if he knew about the Alaska shooting. I explained

40

my head wound as a hunting accident and made no mention of Frank Carter's death – I'd tripped and shot myself, I said. But I did mention the flashbacks, the blaring bugles in the snow, the moose in the clearing that I saw as a Viet Cong guerrilla, memories obviously related to combat experiences. And I told him about my reaction to the family in the Jacuzzi aboard the Stardancer when I'd nearly passed out at the sight of them.

"You said you'd been exercising," he observed. "Not a very bright thing to do when you have a head injury, Major. The blood rushing to your head made you dizzy. What else can you tell me?"

He was pumping me and I didn't like it.

"Look, I came here to ask questions, not answer them. If I had the answers I wouldn't be here. I want to know what you've been treating me for. I think it's post-combat stress syndrome, right? Is that why I freak out every now and then? Am I a danger to myself or others? And what's in those pills you gave me? I've figure I've got a right to know those things, Doc. And if that's my medical file you're fiddling with, I'd like to see it. Let me take it home. I'll bring it back Monday. What do you say?"

"I can't do that, Major. It's against regulations. But I can tell you enough to set your mind at ease. Yes, I've been treating you for many years, about ten to be exact. Your problems stem from your experiences in Vietnam. You'd seen a great deal of combat and had been pretty badly shot up. I'm sure you've seen the scars. There are times when you remember unpleasant things, and the pills help you cope. They're like a sedative; they help you relax. I don't think you're a danger to yourself or to others, so long as you take a pill every day. I don't have enough time to spend with you today, but I do want to see you again very soon. We ought to get to the bottom of this amnesia you claim to be suffering. It doesn't sound as if it's a very serious matter; after all, you say you're remembering things as time goes by. We can probably solve your problem in a couple of sessions. Is Wednesday at three o'clock okay with you?"

"I guess it is. But there are some things that can't wait until Wednesday. For instance, do I have family I ought to get in touch with? How about a job? I don't even know if I should get up and go to work on Monday."

"Nothing like that, Major. You have no responsibilities, no job, unless you consider bar-hopping with juvenile delinquents a form of occupation. And you have no family, no one who'd care about you."

"Thanks. You really know how to make a guy feel good about himself."

"You wanted answers," he said with a sneer. "Sometimes it's best not to ask."

"I'll be here on Wednesday anyway. A couple of days ought to give you time to booby-trap the couch."

The angry words were boiling up in me and just slipped out. But the look on his face told me I'd hit a nerve and I was maliciously eager to follow up on it.

"And another thing, Doc. There was another guy involved in that hunting accident. I apparently blew his head off. I trust he wasn't one of your patients, too."

I left him sitting there wearing a stunned expression as I left to rejoin B.J. who was waiting in the parking lot. If I had to deal with psychos, she appealed to me more than that sadist in the white coat. A big motor home had pulled into the lot next to B.J.'s Bug and there was an unsavory looking character leaning in her window. He was dressed like a bum and wore long hair and a beard. If it had been twenty years earlier I'd have taken him for a hippie. His dirty poncho was cinched at the waist with a broad leather belt and tucked in at the small of his back was a wicked looking knife in a beaded scabbard. He showed just a flicker of surprise as I approached, but it passed in an instant. I figured he was one of the regular nuts here outside Ross' office.

"How 'bout you, mister," he snarled menacingly. "Can you spare a buck?"

"You collecting for the Red Cross?"

"Smart-ass son-of-a-bitch."

I was about to deck him when B.J. gave me a frown that said stow it. I got in and we drove off, leaving the panhandler standing in a cloud of exhaust.

"He was harmless," she said. "Just looking for a handout."

"They ought to be more careful who they let in that place."

"He's probably an ex-GI under treatment."

We drove to Original Joe's No. 2 at Fillmore and Chestnut in the Marina District and ordered a plate of lasagna and a glass of red for lunch. B.J. displayed a whale of an appetite and an equally insatiable curiosity about my "condition," as she called it.

"What did the doctor tell you?" she began.

"Nothing. He wants to see me Wednesday."

"Then let me take a crack at it. Let's start with what you do remember, and when I can fill in a gap here and there, I will."

"Okay. I remember San Francisco, pretty well anyway. But it's as if I lived here in another lifetime. You know, déjà vu. The surroundings are familiar, but I can't put myself in the picture. This restaurant, for instance. I know I've been here before, but I can't remember when or with whom."

"With me," she said brightly. "We come here a lot. You always order Joe's Special or lasagna."

"And my apartment – I know that spectacular view. But it seems as if it's someone else's apartment, someone else's chair. I don't seem to fit anywhere; do you understand what I'm saying? It's as if I'm seeing everything through someone else's eyes. Does that make any sense?"

"Not really. Let's try another tack. Do you member your car and where it is?"

"You told me it was in a rented garage somewhere on Union Street not far from the apartment."

"What kind of a car is it?"

"I don't remember."

"It's a 1968 TR-3. You've been restoring it. It even runs now and then, but you're under it more than you're in it. It's up on jack stands, remember?"

"No. I'll go look at it. Maybe it'll help. But I really want to get my hands on that big, fat file on Ross' desk. I know it's my medical file, maybe all of my Army records. It might be a history of my life and I want to read it. Everything would be spelled out there. He's going to have to let me see it Wednesday or I'm going to have to take it away from him. Meanwhile, I can follow up on a few leads."

"Such as…?"

"Such as a magazine report I came across on the death of Gen. Harrison Parks. I know I served with him in Korea and in Vietnam. Have you ever heard me mention him?"

"Never."

"He could hold some important clues to my past."

"Not helpful, presuming he's still dead."

"True. But his daughter's still alive. I'll start with her. She'd have access to her father's personal effects. Maybe he left a photo album, a diary, a scrapbook. Maybe he even wrote his memoirs. I sense that I was close to him for a long time. If he was the nostalgic type he'd likely make reference to the men he served with over the years."

B.J. wanted to go home to wash her hair, but she let me use her car to begin my search for information. The public library had dozens of telephone books on the shelf and I spent the afternoon looking for a listing for Elizabeth Parks/Mahon. I started with the city and then out into the surrounding area. I didn't find any Elizabeth Mahons, but I did find a listing for General Parks in Woodside. His obituary said he had a home there. It was worth a look.

Chapter 6

The general's estate was on a narrow, winding lane off Mountain Home Road. It was perched on top of a hill covered with a golden carpet of sere grass studded with live oak trees. I couldn't get close enough to see the house before running into no-trespassing signs. When I finally did get a glimpse of it, all that was visible was a stone tower rising in the distance. In another half mile I came to a high electric fence and it was clear I would go no further. Some twenty cars and van were parked off the road and a milling crowd of reporters and photographers was being held at bay by a detail of sheriff's deputies in riot gear. I mingled with the members of the press and tried to get a fix on the situation.

"Forget it, buddy. We've been trying to get inside all day. That television crew over there got here at three this morning, not long after the explosion, and claim they shot some footage before the law kicked them out. Nobody else has gotten beyond this fence. They've got a tight lid on this one."

"What blew?" I asked with the sudden sense that the grim reaper was still following me around.

"The TV crew said it looked like the whole place went up. Nothing much now but smoldering rubble and no official statement, despite all the cops and military brass swarming the place."

"Military brass?"

"A bird colonel seems to be in charge, but he must have a dozen or so uniformed officers under his command. I don't know what they're looking for, but this was General Parks' place. He died a couple of months ago. Maybe he kept some explosives as war souvenirs. The ATF's on scene, but it's anyone's guess because nobody's talking."

There were two military helicopters hovering over the property, shooing away TV choppers that were trying to get aerial shots. I decided that if the professional gatecrashers of the press couldn't get inside, an amateur like me had no chance either. So I headed back to town and went directly to B.J.'s apartment.

"Turn on your television," I said. "See if you can find a live news broadcast. There's something big going on at the general's place."

She had no trouble finding the reports. They were on all of the major channels in living color. The news helicopters had gotten some pretty spectacular film before the military intervention. The estate was huge and had been in the news before – they were showing file clips when we tuned in. But the film from early that morning showed incredible devastation. It must have been one helluva charge and seemed to be centered in a pair of outbuildings, a large multi-vehicle garage, the report said, and a former carriage house that had been converted into a guest residence. Both had been leveled. The general's home, some fifty yards away from the blast crater, had burned to the ground, leaving only a massive granite chimney towering over the ruins like a gravestone. Facts were few and far between, but it seemed certain that no one could have survived such an explosion. The search was still underway for the bodies of the general's daughter and her son, who were known to be staying at the estate. Both were presumed to be a home when the place went up. Reporters were busily interviewing demolition experts, architects and engineers and the consensus seemed to be that the equivalent of a half a ton of dynamite would be necessary to cause such damage and that anyone within a hundred yards would have been blown to kingdom come.

We watched the coverage on and off for the rest of the evening and around eleven we got confirmation of my worst fears. They had found parts of two bodies in the rubble of the guesthouse. Forensic tests were scheduled, the news report said, and positive identification was expected within a few days. I didn't have to wait that long. I knew the bodies belonged to Elizabeth Mahon and her son. And I knew there was a good chance I might be the next to die. There were just too many coincidences – the attempt on my life in Alaska, then poor Ferdy and the poisoned olives, now the general's daughter and his grandson just as I got close enough to ask some questions. Somewhere in that Woodside rubble lay clues that might solve my own personal mystery, but I'd never find them now. The only certainty was that I was still on the killer's list and it would be nice to know who was after me and why before I got it too. I spelled out my fears to B.J.

"I think the clues are locked up in that brain of yours, Pete. I saw a movie once where this woman knew something so horrible that she just blocked it out of her mind. I forget now what it was."

She laughed at herself, an endearing little laugh that made me want to hug her. She had picked up a few things at the grocery on the corner and whipped up a chicken sauté for our dinner, complete with mushrooms and french bread and a green salad on the side. She was a good cook and obviously enjoyed it. I couldn't help but think that she'd make some guy a good wife someday, if she weren't so screwed up emotionally. But she'd never find that guy as long as she was involved with me. I told her I'd be doing her a favor by getting out of her life.

"What does that mean?" she asked angrily. "Are you trying to dump me?"

"No, I'm not trying to dump you. I said I think I'm a marked man and I don't want to put your life in jeopardy. You could get hurt hanging around me. Look at the record. I'm living on a bull's-eye and you could get hit by a stray shot."

"I think you're being pretty dramatic, exaggerating the whole thing. You've lost your memory temporarily and so you're filling your empty brain with all sorts of crazy ideas. You didn't even know that woman who got blown up. What possible connection could her death have with you? You didn't call her, did you?"

"No, I didn't want anyone to know I was coming. I thought the general might have left something behind that would be of use to me, that if his daughter was there, maybe she could help me. But before I could get close...boom! That's why I'm worried about you. If you hang around me, you could get hurt, too. Doesn't that make sense?"

"You're spooked, McCauley, I swear you are. Nobody could get through our security gate, and even if they could, would it make sense to walk down eighty-eight steps to kill us and then walk all the way back up again? We're safe here, because escape would be too difficult. Come on and give me a hand with the dishes and the we'll have another glass of wine while I see if I can get your mind off this business."

She had gotten all dressed up in sort of a peasant outfit and she looked great and smelled even better. Her kitchen was just like mine in the apartment below, so small we had to brush against each other every time we moved. I dragged out the dish drying as long as possible just to be close to her. Turns out it wasn't necessary. She had her own ideas of intimacy and they made mine seem naïve by comparison. I put a log on the fire and made myself comfortable on her couch while she poured me a glass of wine, put a tape on the player and cuddled up next to me. Outside it was a fantasy world of lights against a background of black velvet, Christmas in September, all twinkling and bright and unreal. I felt safe for the first time in days as I relaxed and soaked up the music. It was familiar, Beethoven's Sixth, the *Pastoral.*

"I don't want you to worry, Pete," she whispered. "I know you're mixed up, but I wish you'd let me help you get straightened out. After all, that's how we got together, wasn't it? We were both mixed up. I think that's why we got along so well. We leaned on each other and it helped a lot. I know you disapprove sometimes, but it's worked for both of us. Don't knock it. We need each other and that's what makes it good. I won't tie any strings on you; you don't tie

48

any on me. But no dumping. I'd never dump you. You know that, don't you? We come and go as we please, but we're always there for one another. That's the way it is and that's the way it should be. You need me now more than ever, whether you'll admit or not. And Pete, you know how much I need you. Maybe I can help jog something loose in that brain of yours. At least let me try."

She looked up at me and I couldn't resist kissing her. She went limp in my arms and I could tell right away how she planned to jog my memory. I fought against my natural impulses for a while, but realized it was no use. I couldn't reject her without breaking her heart and I couldn't deny my own passions because...well, because I'm human. Before long she stood up there in the firelight and slipped out of her blouse and skirt and sat down on my lap and kissed me again, this time with passionate insistence. I couldn't keep my hands off her and in no time at all she was on top of me. It was clear that this was the way it always had been, ever since she was a kid. This is the way she liked it, just as she had liked it when her father took her on his lap to comfort her. And then one day he probably slipped over that line that divides the animal instincts in all of us from the disciplined, civilized self. That's when inhibitions went out the window, along with all the hard-earned lessons of survival, all the taboos man had created over the millenniums in order to keep the species pure, to keep the human race on the road toward some state of grace. She was a little girl again, a little girl in a woman's body, complete with baby talk and cute little euphemisms. And there was more to come. After the love-making and the delicious release it brought she was full of reassurances that everything would be all right, just the way she probably reassured her father in what must have been his terrible moments of remorse. Then, laughing and gay as an innocent child, she led me into the bathroom for playtime in the shower. We soaped each other's bodies while the warm water sprinkled over us and every so often she looked up to be kissed and to see if she could arouse me

49

again. And when she succeeded it began all over there amidst the steam and warm water, boldly erect with her face close to mine, her eyes searching mine for some glimmer of recollection.

"Yes," I admitted as we sank into bed to sleep. "You rang bells, B.J., wonderful bells. But not the right bells. You'll have to be patient with me."

The story of the massive explosion at the Parks estate was all over the Sunday Chronicle, complete with a lot of sinister speculation. The general, the story said, was rumored to have connections with a shadowy paramilitary unit known as Omega Force which was suspected of providing arms, ammunition and training to right-wing guerrillas battling Marxist regimes in Latin America. Rumor also had it that the retired four-star general ran a training camp in the coastal mountains and that his Woodside estate was not only his headquarters but also an arsenal for all sorts of sophisticated weaponry and a staging area for combat missions south of the border. News photographers with telescopic lenses had taken pictures of what appeared to be bunkers on the general's property and also a helicopter pad. But the articles also pointed out that the general had owned a private chopper and was an arms collector who had his own firing range. In short, the story raised as many questions as it answered. There were plausible explanations for everything except perhaps the size of the blast – and federal investigators weren't talking about that. With the general's daughter dead, I was left with only one source for the information I needed to put my puzzle together: Dr. David Ross.

* * *

B.J. seemed to enjoy lying about naked in bed after a good night's sleep, teasing me and slipping into the baby talk that seemed to go along with her sexual hang-up. I marveled at how young and fresh she looked in the morning, while I seemed to have aged considerably overnight. It's hell to get old, I thought, and while I wasn't exactly immune to her teenybopper temptress routine, I couldn't afford to waste this Sunday. I had to find Ross and shake some answers out of him. Besides, I liked B.J. better when she behaved like a woman. The Baby Doll act was amusing, but only if you could forget that it was the product of a very disturbed mind. I was determined I wasn't going to let her disturb me.

"You're a son-of-a-bitch, McCauley."

"No, I'm just a tired old man who'd like to find out who he is before he dies. And I'm not going to get any younger playing house with you all day."

"But we do it all the time," she pouted.

"You mean we *did* it all the time. It may have been easy enough when I was all doped up without a care in the world, but now I care – I care a lot. I care about who I am and I care about you. I wish I could convince you it's dangerous to be with me."

"We could watch the 49ers' game!"

"Tape it. I'll watch it later."

B.J. called a pal of hers who was on duty at the telephone company and asked her to check Ross' private number in a reverse directory. The address turned out to be the Opera Plaza condominiums on Van Ness near Civic Center. I called a cab and hiked up the eighty-eight steps to wait for it at the top of the hill. It was a beautiful day and the neighborhood was crawling with tourists wondering how to get to Coit Tower. I didn't know exactly what I was going to say to Ross if I found him, but I had to get my hands on my Army records. Everything I wanted to know would be in them, and maybe that was the problem. Maybe he didn't want me to know anything about my past life. Or perhaps getting close to Ross made him a target, too. With my luck I might not even find him alive. I bluffed my way past a rent-a-guard and caught the elevator to the top floor to see who'd answer my ring. It turned out to be a chubby little guy with a red face who peered out at me from behind a chain-locked door.

"He's not in," he said petulantly.

51

"When do you expect him?"

"That's none of your business."

"Say, this is Dr. David Ross we're talking about, right? The Army shrink?"

That got a rise out of him. I wasn't sure why, but he got very upset.

"You can just get out of here!" he shouted. "He only sees patients at his office. You have no business coming here. How did you get in? You're probably as crazy as the rest of them. Now get away from here before I call the police!"

"Take it easy, pal, I'm not one of Ross' loonies. I'm an old buddy of his who happened to be passing through. Dave asked me to look him up if I ever came to San Francisco."

He grew even angrier when he heard that.

"Why don't you try The Leather Shop?" he hissed.

"The Leather Shop? Where is it?"

"Look it up!" he spat, slamming the door in my face. He was really in a snit and I guessed he wasn't happy that his roommate had stepped out on him. The encounter gave me a whole new perspective on Ross, and it might have given me the leverage I needed to pry loose some information.

Chapter 7

The Leather Shop was an S and M joint on Castro Street only a short cab ride from Ross' apartment. The neighborhood was bizarre to say the least. Homosexuality wasn't just a way of life here, it was a circus, a gaudy spectacle designed to shock. To a large extent it succeeded. I couldn't help but feel sorry for some of the denizens who flaunted themselves in front of gawking tourists. Some of the actors in this social tragedy were defiant and vicious, whether by nature or by the cruel accident of birth that had made them the objects of hatred and bigotry. They were like slaves who suddenly had freedom thrust upon them and didn't know how to handle it. But they knew their oppressors, make no mistake about that, and they were determined to thumb their noses at them by making caricatures of themselves. It gave me an uneasy feeling, a sense of fear that had nothing to do with sexual orientation. I felt a real danger here and decided I wouldn't enter The Leather Shop. Instead I took up an inconspicuous position across the street where I could see Ross if he came out. In half an hour he appeared and stepped briskly down the street. I was about to follow him when I noticed someone else emerge from the watering hole. It was the over-aged hippie I'd run into in the parking lot at Letterman. He paused to watch Ross disappear down the street, then slung a small pack over his shoulder and headed in the opposite direction. That linked the two of them as far as I was concerned, and with Ross now vanished I elected to follow the hippie. I knew where I could find Ross later, but this might be my only opportunity to confront the bearded bum. It had to be more than coincidence that they wound up in the same bar. If Ross had some business with him, it might be useful to learn what it was.

The hippie made a couple of brief stops as he went up the street and seemed to be well known among the locals. Then he entered an apartment building and I dodged into a doorway to wait for him to emerge. When half an hour passed with no hippie, I slipped into the foyer to scan the names on the mailboxes. I no more than got a foot in the door when he lowered the boom on me. It was a good, solid blow to the side of the head and since my head was like a bruised melon already it buckled my knees and I collapsed in a heap. He was on me in a flash, that ugly knife of his at my throat.

"Collecting for the Red Cross, Pop?"

"Hey, take it easy. And lay off my lines."

"I ought to waste you, you old bastard. Why are you following me?"

He eased his grip just enough for me to get an arm free and I exploded in a blind fury. I heard the knife go clattering in one direction while he went sailing in the other. I don't remember hitting him, but when my head cleared he was lying unconscious against the wall and blood was running from his nose. His pack had fallen open and a half dozen small bundles of white powder had tumbled out on the tile floor. I knew it must be drugs and I wanted no part of that scene. I shoved the little packages back into the pack and turned to get out of there just as two guys came bursting through the inside door, the smaller one brandishing a gun, and then two more guys slipped in from the street. The hippie was coming around now and I saw him reaching for his knife. I'd bumbled into the middle of a drug deal and there was no way now to get out.

"Was he trying to rip you off, Indian? Was he trying to get your goods?"

The little guy was holding a gun on me and he looked crazy enough to use it, so I carefully raised my hands over my head while his buddy frisked me very thoroughly.

"He's clean. What'll we do with him?"

"Get him out of here," said the hippie they called Indian. "He didn't see anything. Just get him out of here."

"How do you know he's not..."

"He's a mugger. He's been following me for a couple of blocks. Bounce him."

"But he doesn't look like a mugger," said a guy with spiked hair and green lipstick. "He looks like a cop."

"Then check him out," said the hippie. "Strip him."

"Oh, this is going to be fun," said another of the four as they closed in on me. The little guy with the big gun was licking his chops in anticipation. They were on me in a flash and I felt the same panic I'd felt when I first laid eyes on this neighborhood. Their hatred was so fierce it was palpable and it turned frenzied as they tore at my clothes. In a moment I was lying naked on the cold tile of the foyer with two of them holding me down while a third went through my wallet and the little guy with the gun grinned lasciviously. The guy they called Indian was getting nervous.

"Okay, he's clean. Now get him out of here. We don't need this kind of trouble."

"His ID's okay; he's no cop. But what's he doing here? We can't just let him go."

"Why not?" asked the hippie. "He didn't see anything. Let him loose, and if he knows what's good for him he'll burn rubber getting out of here, won't you, old man."

"I'm not looking for trouble," I said.

"Well, sweets, you found it anyway," said the creep with the gun. "Let's work him over."

The situation was beyond the hippie's control and he was sweating it. He didn't know I knew what was in his pack and he sure as hell didn't want me to find out. The two who were holding me down naked on the floor made obscene remarks about my personal endowments and suggested they needed an airing.

"Good idea," said the guy with the gun, tossing me my wallet. "We'll give you sixty seconds to get lost or you get castrated, old man. Understand?"

They hauled me erect, pulled the door open and shoved me out onto the sidewalk. My clothes came flying after me. I grabbed them up as fast as I could and took off down the street amid a chorus of catcalls and the blaring of horns. I didn't see the black and white that cut in front of me at the corner and screeched to a halt. I hit it on a dead run and went sailing over its hood. A cop loomed over me as I lay sprawled in the gutter.

"Where's your horse, Lady Godiva?" he asked, slapping his nightstick in the palm of his hand. "Or are you Lord Godiva in drag?"

It's tough to come up with a smart answer when you're trying to scramble into your jockey shorts while a crowd gathers around you.

"How about getting me out of here before we create a traffic jam," I pleaded. "I want to report an assault and attempted robbery. I could use a lift to the station house."

"You'll get one, sweetheart. Hop right in."

I was booked on charges of disorderly conduct and indecent exposure and used my phone call to put out an SOS to B.J. She was there within an hour to bail me out.

"I warned you this might happen if you didn't take your pills," she scolded. "I can't wait to read about this in the Chronicle in the morning."

"Never mind the wisecracks, let's just get out of here."

I told her everything. I don't know why, but I had to tell someone in order to convince myself I wasn't cracking up. She said she hadn't suspected Ross was "that way," although it didn't surprise her. There still were a lot of closet cases around, despite the number of liberated gays in the city. She found it difficult to make an ominous connection between Ross and the hippie, but conceded that the Indian could be Ross' supplier. The dope packets I described undoubtedly were cocaine, she said, and after all "everybody was doing cocaine." In all she wasn't much help and by then it was after ten o'clock and she had to get up and go to work in the morning. She lucked out on a parking space for her Bug and we walked down the hill toward the apartment admiring the perfume of the Star Jasmine that filled the warm night air. I unlocked the security gate and we walked down the steps. At her door she stopped only long enough to give me a peck on the cheek, then let herself in. I went down the few steps to my own door, pausing a moment to drink in the spectacular view of the bay at night and to fill my lungs with the incredibly invigorating air. I noticed an envelope someone had slipped under my door and stooped to pick it up as I let myself in and snapped on the light. It was a good thing I'd bent over, because at that instant a bullet thudded into the stairway where I had been standing. I dove for the floor, dragging my finger over the light switch, and lay motionless in the dark for a moment. Then I slowly lifted my head and peered over the windowsill. The roof of the warehouse across Sansome Street was a patchwork of light and shadow. Anyone could be hiding there. I'd heard no shot, which meant the sniper had used a silencer. He could have been there all evening waiting for me to return and probably had me in his crosshairs while I was standing there like a dummy sucking in the fresh air. I was lucky. It could have been my last breath. I eased the door shut and remained motionless until in a moment or two the phone rang. I crawled into the living room to answer it.

"Are you okay?" B.J. asked.

"Yeah, I'm okay."

"I didn't see any lights. I was wondering…"

"I'm fine. It's mellow here in the dark. I like the view. Now get to bed. You've got to work in the morning."

"G'night, Pete."

I went into the bedroom and got a pen light out of the nightstand and looked at the envelope that had been tucked under my door. It was a notice of the next meeting of the Telegraph Hill Improvement Association. Maybe I ought to go, I thought. After all, I owed my life to that group. I settled into the easy chair in the living room and sat up for a long time in the dark, studying the rooftop across the way. I could see the glow of light from B.J.'s apartment above me and could hear her moving about for nearly an hour. She had some goofy rock music on her tape player until the lights went off. Then she put on Beethoven and I listened to the soothing strains of the *Pastoral* until I fell asleep.

* * *

Things had been happening so fast I hadn't taken time to thoroughly examine my own quarters. There could be clues here that might bring the past into focus, so I spent Monday morning going through everything I could find, which wasn't much. The small desk at the back of the living room held a few receipts, utility bills and the like, but nothing that revealed much about me. There were no photo albums, scrapbooks, old letters. It seemed that only Dr. David Ross could provide the answers I needed about my past. I didn't like Ross and it galled me to think I had to go through him to get at my Army records. But there was still one stone to turn. I hadn't looked into the garage where I kept the TR-3. There could be a storage area there worth searching.

Near the intersection of Union and Montgomery were several three-story buildings, flats above and garages at street level. I rented one such garage to house my sports car, a handsome, finely tooled machine that had seen better days. It was up on jack stands just as B.J. had said and it was covered with a thin layer of dust, indicating I hadn't worked on it for some time. There was a grease-stained bench along one wall, a professional looking set of tools and little else. I had no inclination to play the mechanic, so I locked up the garage and wandered up to the corner, not really knowing which way to turn, but determined not to waste the intervening hours before my Wednesday appointment with Ross.

As I passed the corner grocery store a guy in an apron gave me a friendly wave and a smile through the cluttered window. I returned his greeting and paused to scan the bulletin board by the door – lost cats, a car for sale, apartments for rent. On a fresh piece of paper that stood out in contrast to the yellowed notes I was startled to read, "McCauley – Call Dan at 985-4521." Assuming the note was for me, I took it and hurried back down to my apartment. "Dan" answered on the first ring.

"That was fast work, Mr. McCauley. I tried reaching you in more conventional ways, but I couldn't get through your security gate. You are Peter J. McCauley, right?"

"Yes, and who are you?"

"Dan Tobin. I'm a private investigator. You're a moldy old file, McCauley, but an open one."

"I've been around here for a while, what took you so long to catch up with me?"

"Your telephone is unlisted and I couldn't find you before because you never left tracks. I found you today because you finally did."

"I don't know what tracks you're talking about."

"I've got good work habits, McCauley. I check the police blotter every day. What the hell, it's a living, right? And I have a good memory for names. Yours was on the blotter this morning, name and address. A law firm wrote to me several years ago, looking for a Peter J. McCauley. If you're the one they're looking for there might be a little something in it for both of us."

"Maybe I don't want to be found."

"I think you will. It's an estate case. You may have an inheritance waiting for you. What say we get together and discuss it?"

"It could be an inheritance, and it could be an outstanding warrant for my arrest. Why should I trust you?"

"Why not? I'm not a cop. And for a guy who runs around naked in the Castro district, I don't think you're a criminal; I think you must be a comedian. Let's talk it over, what do you say?"

"Okay," I said tentatively. "But in a public place with lots of people."

"You are cautious, aren't you? How about John's Grill on Ellis off Powell? I go there all the time. Just ask for me,

Dan Tobin, at the bar. They all know me. Be there around 2 p.m. after the lunch crowd has thinned out. We can have a nice, public chat."

I was wary, but if this guy was telling the truth he might have information about me that I desperately needed. If it turned out to be a case of mistaken identity, I had nothing to lose but a little time.

Chapter 8

I arrived at John's Grill early to get a jump on Tobin. They knew him all right. He was a regular. They said I couldn't miss him, and they were right. The bartender nodded toward the door as Tobin entered and all I saw was a shadow falling over the room. Dan Tobin was a monster of a man. He stood about six feet, six inches and must have weighed over four hundred pounds. He wore topcoat that made him look like a circus tent with a crumpled fedora on top. He was more than disheveled; he looked as if he'd just walked through a tornado.

"Ah, McCauley," he said as I approached him, "I see you came early to check on me. Well, you can see I am who I said I am and I'm not a cop. Let's take a booth so we can talk privately. I can't manage a bar stool and bartenders have big ears."

He picked a booth in the rear of the restaurant and with great effort slid into the seat, which he filled with his bulk. Once he had made himself comfortable, the table was pushed so far my way I had difficulty squeezing in opposite him. Ignoring my plight, he withdrew a handful of dog-eared papers from his coat pocket and spread them on the table, pawing through them with his huge, meaty hands. The waiter came immediately.

"It's my custom to have a drink before lunch, McCauley. What will you have?" Tobin asked.

"A dry martini, straight up and no olive."

The waiter brought Tobin's drink without having to ask – a double grasshopper which the big man eyed greedily.

"It's all I drink," he explained. "I really don't like most alcoholic beverages, and this reminds me more of mint candy than booze. Cheers, McCauley."

61

As with many huge people, Tobin was gentle as a bird. He grasped the stem of his glass between his thumb and index finger and raised it to his lips with his pinky extended. After sipping the frothy mixture he carefully placed the glass on the table and dabbed at his lips with his napkin.

"Ahhh, delicious," he exclaimed. "And now McCauley let's get down to business. We must see if there is any profit in this for either of us."

He had sorted through the papers and extracted a document that he proceeded to read in the muffled tones one uses to scan through irrelevancies in search of a nugget of importance. Most of what I could catch sounded legalistic, something about claims to the estate of a person named Lundgren. Omaha – I distinctly heard him say Omaha. And the sum, $300,000, came through loud and clear accompanied by a glance from Tobin to catch my reaction.

"Now then, here it is – 'Elmer Lundgren's only known heir is a nephew, Capt. Peter J. McCauley of the United States Army, whose last known address was Letterman Hospital, San Francisco, California.' This is dated January 1974. I don't know how old the attorney's information was. Could it be you they're referring to, McCauley? Or are we dealing here with mere coincidence of names?"

"I don't know. I don't think I know anyone named Elmer Lundgren in Omaha. And even if I did, I don't know how I'd prove it." The reference to Letterman was intriguing, but it might require going into my song and dance about amnesia, and I wasn't ready to do that, not yet. Tobin was the detective, let him prove his case.

"Not much help," he said, fishing a faded photograph from among the papers. He held it up to compare the face to my face. "No help at all," he concluded. "Too old by far."

"Who, me or the man in the picture?" I asked, taking the photo he offered. It was a standard military portrait of a young second lieutenant, the kind of shot that's taken just before graduation from Officer Candidate School – the head shaved, the overseas cap squared away, the manly expression. I noticed the insignia, the crossed rifles of the Infantry. But the face wasn't mine. It was all wrong – the eyes, the nose, the cheekbones, the mouth. The man in the photo definitely wasn't me. A face changes over the years, but not that much. I think I was more disappointed than Tobin was.

"Sorry," I said. "Anyone can see that's not me. I guess you're out the finder's fee, and I'm out an inheritance. But never say die, Tobin. You never can tell when another Peter J. McCauley might turn up on the police blotter."

He was looking at me very closely, not to compare a face with a photograph, but as if seeking something deeper.

"I knew the moment I saw you that this was not your photograph, McCauley. But a photograph might not be conclusive evidence anyway. A court would demand more."

"The cops took my fingerprints," I said, holding up a finger to display an obstinate trace of ink. "They could forward them to Omaha and check them against your McCauley's prints. If he was a commissioned officer, the feds must have them."

He took my hand quickly and examined the faded ink stain.

"This is very interesting," he said.

"What is?"

"They *did* take your prints, and I know I read the booking sheet correctly this morning. But when I went back for a second look after you called, your booking sheet had been pulled. There is no record of your arrest."

"Why would they pull it?" I asked.

"I would guess that it's because you have a lot of clout, McCauley – or a very good lawyer. I can't think of any other explanation."

"Some may have clout in this town, Tobin, but not me. I'm a nobody."

"Then perhaps someone is pulling strings for you, and quite effectively."

He was just a big overgrown bloodhound and he'd picked up a scent. He started sniffing around the edges of my story and it didn't take me long to realize that I could use a man of his talents to help me with my own foundering investigation. I let him break me down slowly by answering his questions, feeding him bits and pieces of information and letting him fit those pieces together. By the time we'd finished our steak sandwiches and coffee he knew almost as much about me as I did.

"Yours is the damnedest story I've ever heard," he said. "I can't understand why you just don't go to the authorities with your problem."

"I've got my reasons," I explained. "The Alaska situation could prove sticky. And it's more direct to go through Ross. He's got my military records as well as my medical history, but he's stiffing me. I'll deal with him first. If I strike out, then I'll look elsewhere for help."

"And you see him Wednesday," Tobin mused. "Tell you what I can do. I'll check him out for you. I can get a line on him through my medical sources. I'll also look into the Alaska case. I'm interested to know if charges will be filed. You may need my help more than you think."

"Wait a minute, how do I know I can afford you? And how do you know I'll pay?"

"So far all we're talking about is my time, which may be of dubious value, and a telephone bill. Everything I have to do can be done by phone. But it'll have to wait until after my nap. I always relax after lunch, have for years. One gets exhausted carrying around all this baggage. A few discreet inquiries may bring information that will be helpful to you when you confront Ross. At least it can do no harm. But you must give me your number. It's inefficient communicating by bulletin board."

Tobin's car was in a nearby parking garage, but I turned down his offer of a lift. It was after four o'clock and the traffic was getting thick and frustrating. It was a beautiful afternoon for a walk, so I went down to Grant Avenue and got caught up in the crowd. It felt good to be lost in the anonymity of the masses, mixing with all the other working people, the shoppers and the tourists. There was a sense of safety being lost in a crowd, a chance to forget for the moment the problems that had been nagging at me for days. I had a gut feeling there was no connection between me and that prairie farmer who left his estate to a nephew who happened to have my name. It was a coincidence, nothing more, or at least I thought so until a strange thing happened that gave me second thoughts. It was something that could have happened to anyone, being mistaken for someone else. But when you're struggling to find out who you are, it can be a jarring experience. I was at the intersection of Grant Avenue and Bush Street, waiting for the light to change. When it flashed green, the crowds on either side of the avenue converged in the center of the street. It was there that someone caught my arm and spun me around.

"Paul! Is it really you?"

He was a sharp dresser, Brooks Brothers type, briefcase, conservative tie. He was younger than I, maybe forty-five, medium height, athletic build, glasses. My first reaction was a mild embarrassment as he stood staring at me through thick lenses.

"Sorry," I said. "The name's not Paul."

He seemed flustered, vaguely disappointed. The amber lights came on and we scurried the rest of the way across the intersection in opposite directions. I paused at the curb and turned to look his way. He had paused, too, and was looking at me with a puzzled expression.

The episode spooked me. Maybe I was Paul – Paul somebody. The name bounced around in the vacant chambers of my mind and I paused to stare at my reflection in a store window, rolling the name over and over, trying to match it with a face, a last name. It was no use. Nothing clicked. I went through the Chinese arch and up the hill into the heart of Chinatown at a brisk pace until I was deep into that other world the Celestials had created there in the midst of this polyglot metropolis. The sights and smells were all familiar. I'd walked this way many times before, I was certain of it. But I couldn't shake that disembodied feeling, as if it were someone else actually plodding along these streets, someone else brushing through the crowd, someone else slowly being swallowed up in a sea of Asian faces. I couldn't shake the thought that maybe I was Paul. But Paul who? And where'd Pete McCauley fit in? Did I have a twin brother, an alter ego? The more I dwelled on it, the more paranoid I became. Every face in the crowd suddenly seemed threatening. It was like being behind enemy lines, surrounded and outnumbered. They were closing in on me and my impulse was to run, to get out of there as fast as I could. Horns honked and brakes squealed as I charged across Columbus in a mad dash to escape. By the time I reached Union Street and turned up the hill for home my head was pounding and my chest ached and I couldn't suck in enough air to keep going. In a panic I collapsed, unable to go on. I tried to scream for help, but no breath came out of my aching lungs. Then I felt an arm around my shoulder, trying to lift me up. I felt relieved, thinking it was all over. I thought I might be feeling Death's grasp, that at last I'd come to the end of the line. I was wringing wet, icy cold and trembling uncontrollably. My head seemed about to explode. I saw brilliant orange flashes in the darkness and I cringed with each blast, weeping with fear. And then I heard a voice.

"Jesus, McCauley! You know you can be down right embarrassing? Get up and let's get out of here before the cops pick you up. God, I can't leave you alone for a minute. What in hell am I going to do with you?"

B.J. got me back to my apartment and into bed and had slipped me a pill before I had enough presence of mind to resist. I don't know if the pill caused the hallucinations that followed, or if the pill came too late to prevent the flashback, but it was the beginning of what seemed like hours of terror, murder and mayhem. At one point the horror of it all sent me smashing against the wall and trying to claw my way out.

Then at last it was over and I collapsed on my bed, my head spinning. I felt I was falling through space, not in fear but with a sense of exhilaration and relief. In the midst of that euphoria I heard Beethoven again and I lay in a meadow bright with summer sunlight, lulled by the song of a meadowlark and cooled by a gentle breeze. I slept the clock around. It was Dan Tobin's call that awakened me around noon.

"Did I get you up, McCauley? You must have had quite a night."

"It *was* quite a night, and I spent it right here in my bedroom."

"What you do in your bedroom is strictly your business. I just wanted to set your mind at rest about the Alaska incident as you called it."

"What was the ruling, accidental death?"

"There was no ruling, McCauley. There was no shooting, no body, no sheriff, no inquest. There is indeed a place called Campbell Lodge, but no one there ever heard of you or a shooting – other than an occasional caribou. My guess is you imagined the whole thing or were the victim of an elaborate charade."

"That's impossible. It wasn't my imagination or a charade that lifted my scalp. And a man did die up there, I'm sure of it."

"Did you see the body?"

"No, I didn't. But they told me Frank Carter was dead and that I killed him."

"Did you know anyone named Frank Carter? Was he a friend of yours? Would you recognize him if he walked through your front door at this very moment? I don't think so. I don't believe you killed anyone in Alaska."

"I don't understand. Did I dream it all?"

"I don't know the answer to that. But I know there is no case against you anywhere in the state of Alaska. Your record is as clean there as it is in San Francisco."

"You think there may be a connection between the two events?"

"I think it's more than a coincidence that you may have run afoul of the law in both places, and that neither has a record of it. Either you're a very important man, McCauley, or a very lucky one. It shall be interesting to find out which it is."

"You plan to stick with it then?"

"Oh, of course, now that my curiosity has been piqued. By the way, I can tell you something about your Doctor Ross."

"Something that might help me get my records from him? Anything I could use to blackmail him?"

"I wouldn't advise that. It's against the law, you know. Although you probably could get away with it, given your relationship with the law. However, there isn't enough on him to support blackmail. He leads an exemplary life. He has an office in Burlingame and lives in Belmont. His wife works part time as a teller at the Bank of America. She went to work last year when their only child, a daughter, went away to school. He's a veteran of Vietnam and an active reservist who puts in one day a week at Letterman counseling veterans with problems such as yours. He was engaged in research there until he retired from active duty in 1980. He goes back there now mainly to keep in touch with his patients. He's a member of the AMA and several golf clubs where he plays occasionally and not very well. He is a member of the First Church of Christ Militant and serves on the vestry. He's a former member of the executive board of the United Appeal. He has a small but elite clientele among the cream of Peninsula society. They pay him $500 an hour for his counsel. He supplements his income with a tidy retirement check from the federal government, the amount of which is based on the highest rank held during his twenty years of service, that of lieutenant colonel. All in all he seems to be an admirable human being, wouldn't you agree?"

"What about his chubby little roommate in the Opera House Plaza apartments and his forays into the S and M scene in the Castro?"

"I'm usually the first to think ill of a man, McCauley, but did it occur to you that both could be explained by his profession?"

"A psychiatrist who makes house calls? Don't make me laugh."

"I'll admit it sounds strange, but some things just can't be properly researched by telephone. They require some legwork. Do you want me to continue?"

"No, you've already told me more than I want to know about Ross. You'd be better off investigating me."

"I really should. Your case intrigues me."

"Forget it Tobin. There's no percentage in it. I can't afford you. And the way things are turning out, I'm not sure I want to know much more about myself. I don't think I'll like what turns up."

"Whatever you say, McCauley. But there is one more item that might bear investigating – Ross' friend at the Opera Plaza. I could make a few calls…"

Tobin was going to keep on my case, whether I wanted him to or not.

Chapter 9

I got another call before I could finish showering and dressing. It was from Inspector Glen Kohler of the SFPD who wanted to see me at my earliest convenience.

"Like this morning," as he put it. "We've got some questions for you."

"I've got a few of my own," I said. "See you in an hour."

Kohler didn't look like a cop. He looked like a stockbroker or a business executive. He would have fit right into the scene on Montgomery Street. He was tall, sharply dressed and neatly groomed. He was a rangy guy in his late thirties, broad shoulders and muscular with a touch of gray in his hair. The only thing that set him apart from those who work in more prosaic occupations was a horrendous black eye.

"Sit down, McCauley. We want to talk to you about Dr. David Ross. What can you tell us about him?"

"He's a psychiatrist. I've got an appointment with him tomorrow."

Kohler ran his fingers through his neatly clipped hair, rummaging around in his imagination for a question that might elicit a more informative response.

"How long have you been seeing him and why?"

"You may not believe this, but I'm not sure. As far as I can honestly recall I've seen him only once in his professional capacity. That was last Saturday at his office at Letterman. But I've been told he's been treating me for years – something about problems related to my military service."

"You don't sound very sure of yourself."

"I suffered a head injury about two weeks ago," I explained, pointing to the angry red scar at my hairline. "I haven't been sure about anything since then. I'm trying to put it all together now. That's why I'm seeing him tomorrow. Why do you want to know?"

"Let's just say we're interested in both of you. Only we don't want Ross to know. We think you might be helpful in that regard."

"Is that why my booking sheet disappeared? Is this a trade-off?"

"I can tell you that the two are related, but I'm in no position to offer you a trade-off. We don't make deals. We do want you to help us."

"How?"

"You've shown a peculiar interest in Ross, and you have a continuing relationship with him. That could be helpful."

"What do you mean, 'peculiar interest'?"

"Come on, McCauley, we know you saw Ross this weekend and that you followed him to the Castro District on Sunday and we both know you got busted there. We want to know why you tailed him. We want to know anything you can tell us about him. And we want you to find out more."

If Kohler knew about my meeting Saturday with Ross and about the Castro incident, where I had made no contact with Ross, it could only mean that Kohler or one of his people was at both scenes. And the only person I knew who was at both scenes was the hippie that the Castro punks called Indian. It didn't take long to figure out who gave Kohler that shiner and why he felt I owed him a favor. Not only had I punched him out, apparently I'd also blown his cover.

"We've been working our way closer to Ross for over a year," he explained. "We were chugging along pretty well before you stepped in and derailed our investigation. We thought it only fair that you help us get back on track."

He didn't sound like he was asking for a favor. There was the sound of "or else" in his voice and I knew I didn't have any options. But maybe we could help each other.

"I'll do whatever I can. I guess I owe you that much. After all, you did keep those creeps from cutting me up. Then there's that shiner I gave you..."

He shifted uncomfortably. He didn't like being found out.

"I said no deals. I can't do a thing for you."

"How about trading information? Run a check on my fingerprints and let me know what you find."

"That's easy. We already did. You're not in our computers. So far as we're concerned, you're clean."

"Did you send them to Washington?"

"We ran them all the way up the line. There's nothing."

That didn't make sense. Peter J. McCauley was a retired Army officer. His prints should be on file somewhere at the federal level – *his* prints, but not necessarily my prints. I began to wonder if it was McCauley who had died up there in the snow – Frank Carter hiding behind the name McCauley. That might explain why they were trying to kill me, whoever "they" were. I decided to go along with Kohler's demands, if only to find answers to my own questions.

"Okay, I'll play along, but put me in the picture. What am I looking for?"

Kohler said they'd pegged Ross as a cocaine dealer, had no trouble discovering where he sold the stuff, but had hit a dead-end when they tried to find out where he got the goods and what he did with the profits. His reputation was impeccable, just as Tobin had said. But he had to have some pretty unsavory friends somewhere along the line. That's where I might be able to help. Keep close to Ross, Kohler told me, and keep SFPD informed of everything I could learn about him.

"That might be tough to do," I pointed out. "I'm the patient; he's sitting in the catbird seat. I may form hunches about Ross, but you're looking for facts. Lately my hunches haven't been panning out."

"What we need is someone who sees Ross regularly, someone he wouldn't suspect was an informant. Even your hunches might be helpful. Let us check them out and decide whether they amount to anything."

"But in checking them out you might blow my cover like I blew yours. It was a hunch that sent me hot-footing it after you on Sunday."

"Get what you can, McCauley. And leave your number with me. I'll be in touch."

I didn't tell B.J. about my involvement with the cops. She was dependent on Ross for her therapy and might not take kindly to my helping pin a drug rap on him. She was home at five-thirty, knocking at my door. She had stopped at Speedy's, the corner market, and wanted to fix dinner for me, or so she said. She really wanted to know how I survived the night.

"It was pretty wild," I admitted. "Do I get that way often?"

"No, not often. You usually take your pills. You scared the hell out of me, McCauley. I've never seen you that bad before."

"Sorry, but I'm not taking those damned pills again until Ross tells me what's in them and why I'm taking them."

"I don't think it's a big mystery. It's probably a downer of some sort, no big deal."

Her offhand manner made me sore. She was a member of the new pill-popping generation, looking for easy solutions, immediate gratification.

"How come you know so much about it?" I challenged her. "And who made you my keeper."

"Don't piss me off, McCauley. You've got no right to talk that way. I try to help you because I like you. We used to get along fine, when you were behaving yourself. Now, I don't know. You're on edge all the time. I never know what you'll do next. We're supposed to help each other, not fight all the time."

73

I'd touched a nerve and she was genuinely hurt. There were tears in her eyes. I took her in my arms and comforted her the way a father might do – and that was just what the doctor ordered. She needed that fatherly touch badly. It was an addiction, a psychological dependency, and it was unsettling as hell. I had a good idea where this bit of affection would lead, and I was right.

"I'm sorry, McCauley, really I am," she sobbed. "I don't know why I let you tick me off so. I know you've got problems and I hate myself for being so selfish."

"Forget it, kid. I'm the one to blame."

"No, I've been bad and I need a spanking, and you know it."

She'd slipped into her Baby Doll mode and the transformation was spooky. She was a different person – coy, manipulative and sexy as hell. I tried vainly to put her off.

"Come on, you're a big girl now," I said, trying to snap her out of it.

"Yeah, and the bigger I get the more I like it. Come on, I need a good spanking, you know I do."

It was another one of her little games and a real turn-on for her, with a lot of giggling and screaming and chasing about. It was a playground game of keep-away with her body as the prize and I fell into the spirit of the game despite my reservations. I tried to catch her to paddle her, but she squirmed out of my grip and dodged away from me, kicking off her shoes as she went. Each time I caught hold of her something gave way – her blouse, her skirt, her bra – until she'd teased me all the way into the bedroom where the game, which was deadly serious by now, was to play itself out. There was fire in her eyes as she backed away from me, egging me on, the perspiration hot on her brow and her cheeks aglow with the thrill of the chase. The bed was between us and she was daring me to come and get her. When I hesitated she climbed onto the bed on her knees, tempting me, flaunting her nakedness and edging closer until

I could reach out and grab her and fling her across my lap. She screamed and laughed as I slapped her silky behind with the flat of my hand and the harder I hit her the quieter she got until her reflexes became slow and rhythmic and her cries changed to deep, erotic moans of perverse pleasure. To see her this way was eerie but irresistible, exciting for me as well. I left off the spanking and began a gentle massage that soon had her writhing in my arms and tearing at my clothes. She was so intense, so deeply enraptured with the act of making love that she wept out loud and tears ran down her cheeks. When we were through she wrapped herself around me like a boa constrictor and squeezed me so tight I could barely breathe. She thanked me over and over again as if I'd bestowed the gift of life on her. The whole routine exhausted me emotionally and physically. I ran it over in my mind and I could see her as a little girl with her playmates in innocent merriment and it saddened me to think how twisted it had all become. I began feeling remorseful when mercifully I fell into a deep sleep. When I awakened I heard the shower running and I was glad I'd avoided the warm water encore. I don't think I could have made it.

She did a stir-fry for dinner, fish and chopped vegetables, and I cracked a bottle of fume blank. She was a completely different person, happy, chattering about irrelevancies, laughing spontaneously as she stood there in one of my shirts that hung to her knees. She was barefooted, her hair wet and pulled back in a makeshift ponytail, and she was lovely to look at. She ate hungrily, hardly touching her wine, and talked incessantly through dinner. It gave me a feeling of listening to a daughter just home from school. It was as if the spanking episode had never happened. She made no reference to it until she decided to go. Then, as she collected her things that were scattered all over the apartment, she summed it up with a flip comment.

"You're pretty tough on a working girl's wardrobe, Pete."

"And you're tough on an old man's, uh, constitution," I said.

"Not too old. I'd give you a reference anytime."

Then a quick peck on the cheek and she was gone and I was left with the sudden realization that we'd been sitting there in my window under a bright light all through dinner. We'd been perfect targets for anyone who might want to snipe at us from across the way. It was dark and there was no telling what might be lurking on the roof of the warehouse across the street. I lowered my blinds and stretched out on my bed to read myself to sleep. There was a follow-up story in the newspaper about the explosion and fire at General Parks' estate, accompanied by mug shots of the general's daughter, Elizabeth Mahon, and her son who had both died in the blast. She had worn a veil in the photograph taken at her father's funeral, but this was a studio portrait and she was a real beauty. I remembered reading that Parks had married a Japanese woman while stationed in Tokyo before the Korean war and their daughter obviously had inherited her mother's delicate bone structure, the high cheekbones and the almond-shaped eyes. Her son, a handsome lad in his late teens, in turn had fallen heir to his mother's best features. They were two very beautiful people and their deaths seemed such a terrible waste. I read the article through, then went back over it carefully. It was fascinating. Old Hell-for-Leather Harry had become a super patriot after his retirement, it said. He headed a paramilitary organization called Omega Force and had taken it to Central America on several occasions to train guerrilla units whose aim was to overthrow Marxist governments. The Americans were strictly non-combatants and carried on their activities with private funds and a wink and a nod from the administration. The article also said the law had found no clues to the tragedy at the estate, or at least none that anyone would talk about. I began to mull over several possible scenarios, but it had been a long day and I couldn't hold my eyes open very long. I flicked out the light and dreamed not about bloody

76

combat or exploding mansions, but about schoolyard games in which I chased after pretty girls. One was dressed in a man's shirt. She had dark hair and an infectious laugh. When I caught her at last, the shirt tore away and she stood naked before me. It wasn't B.J., it was Elizabeth Mahon, her delicate body terribly burned. The shock awakened me and I lay there for a long time wondering what the Army shrink would make of it all.

Chapter 10

I took a cab to Letterman the next afternoon and found Ross ready and waiting. He worked without a receptionist or nurse, answering my knock himself and ushering me into the semi-darkness of his inner sanctum.

"I thought it best to get right down to business, Major McCauley. You don't mind, do you? This aberration took me by surprise and I want to get to the bottom of it as quickly as we can. I've got too many years of work tied up in you to let a simple blow to the head undo it all. Why don't you sit down here and relax and I'll get started with a couple of questions. You may elaborate on your answers however you see fit."

"Look, Doc, I don't mean to be telling you how to run your business, but I'd like to lead off with a few questions first. It would help if I knew how I came to be your patient and when. Who am I, what's wrong with me and what are you doing about it?"

"Fair questions," he allowed after a moment's pause. "I'll start with the basics. You're Major Peter J. McCauley, retired. You spent more than twenty years in the U.S. Army, Infantry. You were a combat officer in Vietnam when you first started having problems. You were wounded and rotated back to the states, where you were promoted to your current rank while still hospitalized. You were awarded the Purple Heart and a Bronze Star with two oak leaf clusters. You were released from the hospital in 1970 and returned to duty as a training officer at Fort Ord. Later that same year you were sent to me suffering from a delayed reaction to your combat experiences. You were frequently disoriented, occasionally hallucinatory, and at least once you were suicidal. In short, you were very near the edge. You were assigned to my care because post-combat stress syndrome is my specialty. I'd had a great deal of success dealing with cases such as yours. I'd had my share of failures, too. It was not a pretty war and it didn't do pretty things to people. Fortunately you were one of my success stories – until your recent injury. I don't know what effect it will have on your therapy. Amnesia is not uncommon in cases like yours. It's a game your brain plays to avoid dealing with unpleasantness. But yours is unusual, the result of induced traumatic insult apparently unrelated to your combat experiences. But amnesia is treatable. Whatever its origins, it can be dealt with in therapy."

First impressions are hard to shake and I couldn't shake the negative vibes I got from Ross. So far he hadn't told me anything I hadn't already figured out and I was impatient to get deeper into my background.

"I've had a couple of flashbacks in recent days, Doc. They're quite real and quite ugly. And they all seem to relate to combat. But let's face it, I wasn't born and raised in the Infantry. I must have had a life before Vietnam, before the Army. I want to know about my life before all that. Who am I? Where was I born? Who were my parents? I want to know the really basic things about my life. I'm sure the answers are there in my military records and I'd like to look at them."

He flipped through the pages of my file, adjusting the glasses that had slipped down his nose.

"There's not much verifiable material here," he answered vaguely. "But I can tell you what you told me when we started your therapy back in the 'seventies. You said you were born in 1933 in Omaha, Nebraska. You were an only child, orphaned in early 1950 just before graduating from high school. Your parents were killed in an automobile accident in February of that year. You managed to support yourself briefly as a grocery store clerk until you graduated. You enlisted in the Army in September, went through basic training at Fort Riley, Kansas, and were sent to Korea as a private first class. You were assigned to the First Cavalry Division and promoted very quickly, presumably because your division suffered a high degree of casualties. You eventually earned a battlefield commission and returned to the states as a first lieutenant. You spent some time in the NATO command and, let's see – yes, later on you were sent to Vietnam as a member of an advisory unit. You later served as commander of a line company."

He skipped a few pages, scanning them quickly and moving on.

"We've already touched on your medical history. I've been seeing you on an outpatient basis for more than ten years. You've had a good record of recovery, with only occasional relapses. You've been capable of holding down a job for many years but have chosen not to work. Your retirement and disability pay apparently have been sufficient to satisfy your needs. There's nothing in your records to indicate next of kin. As a matter of fact about a year ago you had your GI insurance changed to appoint Barbara Jean Franklin as your beneficiary, no relationship indicated."

The tone of his voice told me he thoroughly disapproved of my lifestyle, particularly my relationship with B.J. I thought this was strange, because B.J. led me to believe he had encouraged it.

"How about B.J.?" I asked. "She seems to be my official keeper and I get the idea that you put her up to it. She's your patient, too, isn't she? Didn't you bring us together?"

"I'm not at liberty to discuss Miss Franklin's case with you, Major. It is immaterial anyway. She is not the reason for your being here. You're looking for help in curing a mild case of amnesia. I am convinced that we need only pick up your therapy where we left off several weeks ago..."

"Tell me about my therapy," I interrupted. "Why the pills?"

"Your therapy involves a combination of hypnosis and mild doses of barbiturates. The hypnosis helps you come to grips with your past, the pills help you to cope with present. As for Miss Franklin, I can only tell you what you already know: you are neighbors who happen to be patients here. If interdependency has developed between you, I certainly

80

didn't encourage it, although I don't necessarily disapprove so long as it remains within bounds. It can be therapeutic to have a shoulder to lean on, particularly if it's reciprocal."

"It's not an even match, Doc. She nags me into taking my pills, while I seem to be on call for stud services. I don't see how that could be therapeutic for either of us."

"Moral judgments aside, I'd have to agree with you. Miss Franklin is outwardly a very normal young woman. Inwardly she's a very confused child. I will not venture to characterize your mental state, except to say that what you and Miss Franklin do *for* one another could be helpful; what you do *to* one another is definitely not. But unless your relationship becomes intrusive, it is of little concern to me. In short, if it feels good, do it; if it doesn't, then you must stop."

It wasn't difficult to understand why Ross had such a lucrative practice among the country club set. That was the kind of prescription that could justify any sort of behavior this side of Sodom and Gomorrah. But it wasn't getting me any closer to the answers I wanted. He seemed to sense my impatience and launched the therapy session. He dimmed the lights and hit a button with his foot that sent soft music wafting from speakers mounted high on the walls. Not surprisingly, it was Beethoven's Sixth Symphony, the *Pastoral*. I recognized every phrase, every movement. It obviously had been a part of my treatment for years. Music to sooth the savage breast, only in my case it had been planted deep in my subconscious through hypnotism. That step was next. Ross donned a headband with a tiny light affixed and beamed it directly at my eyes, at the same time speaking very, very softly above the music.

"Don't look directly at the light, Major. Look at this pendant, watch it move from side to side. Don't turn your head; follow it with your eyes. See how it slowly swings from left to right. That's it, keep your eyes on it and let your mind go blank. Relax. Let yourself go. You will feel yourself sinking slowly, quietly to rest. Now you're floating

81

effortlessly through space. You are free as a bird. Take a deep breath. Feel your eyelids grow heavy."

The light formed a halo around the swinging pendant, obscuring everything else in the room. It was a curious object, like a tiny horseshoe. As I watched it swing I felt myself sinking toward a deep sleep, until I consciously resisted, shaking myself awake and shielding my eyes.

"Well, I see that you're fighting me," Ross said indignantly. "I cannot hypnotize you against your will. Remember that this therapy is only as effective as you make it. If you fail to cooperate, I can't help you. But let me assure you that hypnosis is much more pleasant than those flashbacks you've been experiencing. If you want to get to the root of your problem, we'll have to try again. You must be mentally prepared to cooperate. Let's try again next week – Wednesday, same time. All right?"

I was a little woozy from the experience and it took a moment for his words to register. The music suddenly stopped and the lights came on and he was reaching in a cabinet from which he extracted a small bottle of pills.

"Wednesday, three o'clock," he repeated. "Can you be here?"

"Yes, yes, sure." I had that odd, disembodied feeling that had come over me several times recently. I seemed to be outside myself, hovering over the scene but not really experiencing it, not feeling a part of it. He handed me the pills.

"One a day at bedtime," he said. "It's a mild sedative. It'll bring you pleasant dreams. If you experience any more flashbacks, try to remember what they are about. Write them down. Next week we'll talk about them and try to break down a few barriers. I think you may be more receptive then and we can make some progress."

I came away from the session with nothing to pass on to Kohler, and little better off myself. I did have the pills; they could be a clue. And Ross had confirmed there indeed was an Omaha connection. It was probably just a coincidence, but I could pass it on to Tobin and let him chew on it. All was not lost so long as Tobin was still on my case. His big Oldsmobile was wedged in the small turnaround on Calhoun Terrace when I got back to Telegraph Hill and he had worked himself into a lather trying to extricate it.

"McCauley, this is the god-damnedest cul-de-sac in San Francisco. Get me out of here, will you?"

"How'd you manage this, Tobin? I may have to hire a crane to lift you out."

He struggled from behind the steering wheel and after some careful maneuvering I managed to get the big car turned around and pointing uphill toward freedom. I invited him down to my apartment for a cold beer, but when he found out it was at the bottom of eighty-eight steps, he declined.

"Let's stand here and enjoy the view," he said. "I'm afraid I couldn't get down those steps, much less get back up again. I've got some information about Ross' boyfriend. He's Conrad Peabody III, Connie to his friends, scion of an old San Francisco family."

"Good for him, but what in hell does it mean?"

"You've undoubtedly heard of the Peabody Lines, founded by his great-great-grandfather in the days of the clipper ships. He bought his first sailing vessel with the gold he'd panned in the Sierra foothills in 1850. He was a tough old buzzard who skippered that ship himself. He sailed it in the island trade initially, eventually built a fleet of sailing ships and lived long enough to establish a line of more than twenty steamships engaged in worldwide trade. His only son was a drunk, so the old man left it all to his grandson, Connie's father, who lost most of it in the crash of 'twenty-nine. There wasn't much left for little Connie after his father took a header from the 12th floor of the Peabody Building onto Montgomery Street – except the Peabody Building itself and a half dozen other pieces of choice real estate in downtown San Francisco. The result – Connie III is a very wealthy young fellow."

83

"That's strange. Why does Ross have to sell cocaine when he's got a rich buddy like Peabody and a lucrative medical practice to boot? It just doesn't fit."

"Several reasons come to mind. First, he might have an expensive habit himself and not want his own bank account to reflect it. Second, he may have other expensive habits that have nothing to do with drugs – he may be an art collector, for example, or a compulsive gambler. He may dabble in antiques or maybe he's an embezzler trying to cover up his theft before it's discovered. It could be anything. A man with an obsession might go to any lengths. It bears looking into, don't you think?"

"You're going to keep right on with it, aren't you, Tobin? I warned you I might not be able to afford your fee."

"Nonsense, McCauley. Everything I just told you I got from the public library in a couple of hours of research through their microfilm. Does that sound expensive?"

"I won't know until I get your bill, will I?"

"You'll find that I come cheap when I'm enjoying myself, McCauley, and I'm enjoying this case. It baffles me and I can't stand to be baffled. There's an explanation for everything, and I'll get to the bottom of this mess, of that you can be sure."

"Then let me throw you another bone. I had a session with Ross today and got him to open my Army records. Among other things, the records say I'm an orphan from Omaha. Maybe you'll be able to claim that finder's fee yet."

"That's interesting and certainly worth pursuing. But we still face the problem of establishing your identity if we're to collect any of that $300,000. Did your records indicate anything about your family, for example."

"Not much. I supposedly told Ross early on that my parents died in an automobile accident in 1950. But there were no names, no addresses."

"I think that's enough to get started. Presuming you bear your parents' name, I can take that snippet of information and expand on it."

"And while you do, I'll have another go at Peabody."

"You may find him on Jackson Street just off the square. He's the proprietor of a decorator's shop, a wholesale operation. Not surprisingly, it's called Peabody's. You can't miss it. It's one of those old warehouses that have been converted into shops. Very chic. He owns the building and several others nearby. It might be a starting point, possibly a front for some illicit operation, importation of stolen objets d'art, perhaps. Such an enterprise might require the large sums of money that cocaine would bring in."

"You need a good imagination in your business, don't you, Tobin. I never would have thought of Ross as an art smuggler."

"Oh, he probably isn't. Not polished enough, I'd say. But it'll get you thinking like a criminal. You must, you know, if you're going to beat them at their game."

I was certain Tobin would disapprove of my working for the SFPD, so I let him go on his way without telling him about Glen Kohler. And Kohler wouldn't approve of Tobin, either, so I also had to keep him the dark. But there was nothing to prevent me from passing Tobin's information on to Kohler. Besides, I needed a chemical analysis of the pills Ross gave me, and I figured the cops could make a quick job of it in their lab. Kohler wasn't at all impressed.

"I don't know who your sources are, but everything you told me is old hat," he said. "It's easy to check on a man's family, his profession, his social habits. What we want to know about is his criminal activities. Where does he get his stuff, and what does he do with the money he gets for it? That's what we want you to get for us, if you can. You seem to have at least a nodding acquaintance with the criminal element in this town."

"You're wrong, Kohler. You're the only drug dealer I know, and now that you've traded in your hippie beads, where does that leave me?"

"Back with Doctor Ross, where we can't get."

"I'll see if I can do better next time. But you've got to be patient. Remember, he's the hypnotist, not me."

I gave him my pills to analyze, but I kept Conrad Peabody III to myself. If Kohler knew about him, he hadn't let on, and I needed some fresh ground to plow if we were to get to the bottom of this. I walked downtown from Civic Center and met B.J. when she got off work at the telephone company. We stopped at the Fiore d'Italia on Washington Square for dinner on the way home. She wanted to know all about my session with Ross and I told her all I could, which wasn't much. Then we grabbed a cab and whipped around to Pier 23 to listen some great jazz piano until about ten when be both started to drag. It was a beautiful night, so we dodged through the traffic across The Embarcadero and trudged slowly up the Telegraph Hill steps and home. She thanked me, gave me the routine peck on the cheek and reminded me to take my pill before going to bed. I wasn't about to take a pill until I knew what was in it. I was sitting alone in the dark, wondering if Kohler had tried to call me when the telephone rang.

"McCauley?"

"Yes, Kohler, what have you got?"

"I know what you've got," he said.

"Let's have it – what's in the pills?"

"Out of the one hundred pills in the bottle, ninety-four were placebos."

"They're what?"

"Placebos. Sugar pills. Nothing at all."

"What about the other six?"

"They're the same base, only they're laced with lysergic acid diethylamide."

"What the hell is that?"

"Acid, McCauley, LSD. No wonder you've been blowing your gourd. Are you sure you didn't know what he was feeding you?"

"I swear to God I didn't."

"It certainly explains why you've been flipping out."

"Yeah, but it raises another question – why?"

"I'd get back to him, if I were you. A patient's got a right to know about such things. You can't go around polluting people's minds, even if you are a doctor. Lay it on the line, pressure him."

"I want to help you, Kohler, but I don't want to get myself killed in the process. Let me work on this in my own way."

"Whatever you say, but take some advice from a narc – stay away from those pills. They'll stunt your growth."

Chapter 11

Tobin was right when he said I had to think like a crook in order to get the goods on Ross. To be more precise, I had to think like a burglar. The building was not a difficult nut to crack, even for an amateur like me. It was a three-story brick warehouse with decorator showrooms on the ground floor. I walked by it once pretending to inspect the window display and counted the people inside. I could see one salesman in animated discussion with a customer and two men near a desk toward the rear. Around back in the alley I found the service entrance, a big roll-up door that opened onto a freight elevator and a small door marked "Receiving." I paused in the shadows across the alley and waited for an opportunity. At noon the two men I'd seen through the front window came out the small door, closing it carefully behind them and tugging it to make sure it locked. I was thinking about bluffing my way in the front door when a truck entered the alley and pulled up to the freight elevator. One man got out and hoisted the elevator door while the driver jockeyed into position to unload the cargo. As the truckers wrestled the crates aboard the lift, I walked up and shook the doorknob on the small door.

"Damn, I forgot my key," I exclaimed loudly enough for them to hear me. "I'll just cut through here."

I walked through the freight elevator and into the building as if I belonged there and was relieved to see there was no one around. I went quickly to a stairway to the second floor, went up and poked around among the packing cases, not knowing what I was looking for – just something, anything out of the ordinary that might link Ross and his cocaine sideline to Conrad Peabody III. Any of the crates might contain contraband of one sort or another, but without a crowbar there was nothing much I could do. The same was true on the third floor, a dozen or so crates with shipping addresses from all over the world and all of them sealed. I went over to a dusty window that looked down into the alley thinking that I would have made a lousy detective when something familiar caught my eye. It was one of those huge, slope-nosed recreation vehicles with tinted glass windows waiting near the freight elevator. When the delivery truck pulled away the RV drove into the elevator. I was sure it was the same rig I'd seen Saturday in the parking lot at Letterman, the vehicle that was parked next to B.J.'s Bug when I first ran into Kohler in his hippie get-up. I went over to the elevator shaft in time to see the steel doors clang shut. The gate came down with a loud rattle and the elevator started. I was about to duck for cover when I realized the elevator was going down to the basement. Looking into the shaft I could see the RV roll off the lift and out of sight.

I was heading down the stairway for a closer look when the two men who had left earlier returned through the alley door. I flattened myself against the wall, hoping they wouldn't see me, but I needn't have worried. They were too preoccupied with one another to notice much of anything. They seemed to be very good friends, indeed. I'm not a fan of alternative lifestyles, but at least their stolen intimacies prevented them from spotting me. When they finally went their way into the front showrooms, I crept quietly down the stairway to the basement where I found the RV parked in the brightly lit main room. At the far end of the room was a raised stage with a podium and at the near end were two rooms, one with its door ajar. I couldn't see through the RV's tinted window, but figured the rig was empty when I heard laughter coming from the room. Reasoning that whoever had been in the RV was now in that room, I sidled along the wall and peeked in. I was stunned to see Peabody talking to a man I'd seen before – my cruise shipmate, Felkerson. If that wasn't surprise enough, the next thing I felt was the cold muzzle of a weapon on my neck.

"Harold," said a calm voice behind me, "we have a visitor."

Both men came to the door and stared at me in amazement.

"Who is this man and what is he doing here?" Peabody sputtered indignantly.

"It's McCauley," said Felkerson. "I don't know what he's doing here."

"Well, get rid of him and close the door. Say, I've seen you before!" Peabody exclaimed. "You came to my door looking for David."

"He's clean," said the woman with the revolver who had been patting me down.

"Then put the gun away," said Felkerson. "We don't want to attract attention. What in hell brought you here, McCauley? Ross assured us you'd be no trouble."

"He was sneaking up to the door," said the woman. "He was eavesdropping."

"I don't want any trouble," I said. "I just want out of here."

"Not on your life, McCauley, and I mean that literally," Peabody said. "I'm afraid you won't be going anywhere until David claims you. Take him to the storeroom, Mrs. Felkerson," he said, tossing her a key. "And be careful. If he's one of David's psychos he could be dangerous."

She herded me to the next door, unlocked it and prodded me inside with her revolver. After she's slammed the door and locked it from the outside I briefly contemplated my stupidity. She must have been watching my every move from behind the tinted glass of the RV, confirming my earlier conclusion that I'd make a terrible burglar. The big question was, What were the Felkersons doing here? And why the hardware? I looked around the storeroom and saw dozens of folding chairs stacked against the wall. Across the room was a clothing rack filled with red vests on hangers, and on the floor a box full of black armbands. On the back of each vest was a circle with a stylized swastika in the center with a lightning bolt running through it. The same symbol was on each armband. I'd stumbled into the meeting hall of some neo-Nazi organization and apparently Peabody and the Felkersons were a part of it. From the way they spoke of Ross, he was involved, too, and my fate seemed to be in his hands. A stack of pamphlets on a table told me more than I wanted to about these creeps.

They called themselves The Group and this was their western district headquarters. Their propaganda described them as patriots engaged in a struggle for survival against all sorts of enemies. They believed the United States was in the grips of socialism and on the verge of falling under the control of international communism. To prevent the overthrow of the government they advocated warfare against everyone who wasn't white, Anglo-Saxon, Protestant and at least as paranoid and bigoted as they were. The only thing democratic about The Group was their hatred. They hated everybody – Catholics, Jews, Democrats, Republicans, the bench and the bar, and of course the media. They hated blacks, browns, reds and yellows; they hated ban-the-bombers and all other peaceniks. They hated environmentalists and hippies, dopers and druggies. They believed Congress was rife with traitors intent on repealing the Second Amendment in order to facilitate a communist takeover. And to weaken the populace those traitors used a most insidious weapon of all, the dreaded Internal Revenue Service. Even the most upright American citizen was a dupe of the communists if he didn't share their fear of a worldwide plot to destroy individual freedoms. But if The Group hated a lot of things, they professed to love their country with a fanatical, flag-waving fervor. Mrs. Felkerson interrupted my reading.

"Colonel Ross says you're to behave yourself. He wants to see you later tonight. I've brought you something to eat." She handed me a bag from McDonald's.

"Here I am a spit and a holler from Tadich's Grill, and you bring me a Big Mac. This just isn't my day."

91

"You're lucky to get anything at all. When you're through you can help us set up for the meeting."

She talked tough, but she wasn't carrying her revolver. I guessed Ross told them I wouldn't be a problem, so I decided I'd better not be. Ross still held most of the answers I needed, and alienating him now might mean the end of my search for information, and possibly for me. Felkerson himself let me out, ordering me to carry chairs into the main room and set them up in rows facing the stage and podium. Peabody was nowhere to be seen. We made three rows of ten chairs each, and then Mrs. Felkerson set up a table at the foot of the basement stairs while her husband went up to the alley door to screen arrivals for the meeting. They came singly or in pairs, each pausing at Mrs. Felkerson's table to sign in and receive a vest and armband. They were all white, mostly men, young people and old, working stiffs and businessmen, nearly thirty in all. They took their seats and sat quietly until the steel doors of the freight elevator opened and a sleek silver Cadillac limousine rolled into the cavernous basement. With a flourish a chauffeur dismounted and opened the rear passenger door. Out climbed Conrad Peabody III, all dressed up in a khaki uniform with gobs of brass, a hat with a shiny visor and knee length boots polished to a luster. He looked like a mini Hermann Goering with his pudge hanging over his belt and his jowls ajiggle as he swaggered to the stage and took his place behind the podium. He was greeted with respectful silence and a standing salute, each member extending the right arm with fist clenched. The effeminate little wimp was a real fire-eater when it came to rallying the troops. He parroted all the trash I'd read in the pamphlets before he introduced the evening's guest speaker: Col. Harold Felkerson of Omega Force.

Old Hell-for-Leather Harry Parks must be turning in his grave, I thought. According to what I'd read, Parks had fashioned Omega Force as an elite paramilitary unit operating under the auspices of the CIA, and here was Felkerson delivering a recruiting speech to a bunch of free lance fascists. He was looking for a few good men, he told them, healthy young people with a liking for adventure and discipline, preferably men with prior military experience. He spoke of confronting the communist peril at our southern border, conjuring up images of brown hordes swarming over our country, perverting its institutions and mongrelizing the great white race. He raised the specter of rape and pillage and plague, and for his efforts he managed to get three prospective recruits to sign up for training in Omega Force. The assemblage stood quietly at attention as Peabody closed the meeting and departed in his classy car, leaning out his window to give the clenched-fist salute to his followers. Then the Cadillac rolled onto the elevator and rose mystically into the night.

I must have had a wry grin on my face after the Felkersons had ushered out the last of The Group members.

"What's so funny, McCauley?" Felkerson asked.

"Nothing's funny, Felkerson. As a matter of fact, I think it's sad."

They bundled me into the RV and drove to Letterman, where Felkerson, gun in hand, escorted me to Ross' office.

"So you know about Connie," he said after the Felkersons left. "I'd like to know how you found out."

"No mystery," I said. "You gave B.J. your private number and I traced it to Peabody."

"But whatever possessed you to go to that meeting?"

"I'd heard that Hitler was alive and well in Jackson Square and I had to go see for myself. Damned if he isn't! He's put on a little weight..."

"I won't tolerate your snooping, Major! You're butting in where you don't belong."

"I told you I'm looking for answers, Ross, and I'm not above blackmailing you to get what I want. If you're afraid I'll embarrass you, why not tell me what I want to know?"

"I've told you everything."

"Bullshit! There's a lot you're not telling me, like why you're feeding me LSD."

That startled him. His eyes widened and his hands began to shake.

"I had a lab run a test on the pills," I said. "I've got a good mind to turn you in."

"A good mind? That's where you're wrong, McCauley. You don't have a good mind and that's why you won't turn me in. You'll open a can of worms and you'll live to regret it. It would mean the end of everything, for you as well as for me."

"It may mean the end for you, Ross, but it might be a beginning for me."

"Don't be ungrateful. I've given you years of life you otherwise would not have enjoyed. Life is very precious, McCauley, very precious. And you owe yours to me."

"If running around in a hypnotic trance or having LSD fits is your idea of living, you're the one who should be on the couch, Doc. You need therapy more than I do."

"It's too late for that," he said with an ironic smile, "much too late. I'm telling you this because I think that deep down, once you've heard the whole story, you'll agree that I'm right. The fact is the whole house of cards is about to tumble down around us both, unless you can help prevent it. And I know you can."

"So you're in a jam, Ross, and you want me to pull you out?"

"We can help each other," he said, pressing the stereo button that filled the room with the music of Beethoven. He studied my face for a sign, but I gave him none.

"That won't work, Doc. You tried that one already. You said so yourself – you can't hypnotize someone who doesn't cooperate, right?"

"I thought if you relaxed you might be more receptive to what I'm going to tell you. It isn't a nice story. You're not going to like what you hear, but then you weren't a very nice man. I may have been able to save your life, but even I can't work miracles. Let me begin with some information I hope will make you more cooperative. You did kill Frank Carter and I know where the body's buried. While you may turn me in for malpractice, I could turn you in for murder."

Chapter 12

The story Ross told added a lot of pieces to the puzzle and also sent a chill up my spine. He began with his own background. He'd been introduced to works of Freud in college and it gave him a life-long fascination with the functioning of the human mind. He entered medical school during the latter months of World War II and fended off the draft board until he earned a degree in psychiatry. The war was over by then, but there was a great need for his specialty, with hundreds of returning GIs suffering from what then was called battle fatigue. It offered the perfect internship for an eager young draftee like himself and his success record was better than most. He was up on all the latest techniques in psychotherapy and brash enough to try anything to reach his goal.

"And what was your goal?" I asked him.

"Permanent mind alteration," he said. "We tried anything and everything. Eventually the government established a special unit for us. It included a surgical team that experimented with lobotomies. It was pure research at the highest level – using human beings as our subjects. Our patients were a sorry lot, men who had nothing to lose. If they didn't submit to our experimentation, the alternative was to spend the rest of their lives in mental hospitals. It was easy to persuade them or their families to cooperate."

"Brain surgery, mind alteration – it sounds like risky business," I said.

"Not every experiment succeeded, of course, but there are surprisingly few failures around today as evidence. Remember that our work went on for years. Families and loved ones give up easily as the months drag on. They didn't want to be troubled with the mental invalids. They didn't want to be reminded of the war and its terrible toll. The world was moving on and they didn't want to be left behind with nothing but the heartbreak and misery of the past. Most were content to leave the human debris of war for us to clean up. They found it liberating to sign medical release papers. It allowed them to forget, and many of them never looked back."

It was clear that Ross was intent on pursuing this impromptu examination of his own past, and insofar as it offered broad insights into my predicament, I let him proceed, even encouraged him at times. It was as if we'd changed places, with his life under the microscope, not mine. He sat at his desk in the near darkness, fingering the horseshoe-shaped trinket he had used to hypnotize me, lost in the clouds of his past.

"We made great strides during the years immediately following the war, but it was later, after the Korean conflict, that we faced our greatest challenge. We'd been out of touch with the Chinese for years and we discovered they were far ahead of us in many respects. We had no idea just how advanced they were until our prisoners of war began returning and the term brain washing entered our vocabulary. We quickly began playing catch-up. The government ordered us to master the Chinese techniques and to develop counter-therapies. We were experts ourselves by the time the Vietnam War evolved, but by then the government's priorities had changed. Our research group began to fall apart. Older officers retired, younger ones drifted off into private practice where there was big money to be made by anyone with a quiet office and a couch. A select few of us, however, were offered a new opportunity. We had done some of the pioneering work with mind-altering drugs and had achieved a degree of success that caught the eye of the Central Intelligence Agency. Eventually we were placed under the agency's control and put to work in its MK-Ultra program. Since most of our research involved drug experimentation, it had to remain top secret. Many of our GIs were returning from Vietnam hooked on heroin and cocaine. Drugs were rampant in society, from crack heads in the slums to pot heads on our school grounds to coke sniffers in our executive suites. Young Americans were spacing out in the streets, a fact brought home to us every night in television news reports. Everyone was drug conscious. If the public had known its government was experimenting with some of those same drugs, there would have been a horrendous outcry. We had to remain under cover."

"Why the emphasis on mind control?" I asked.

Ross pondered the question for moment, then raised his eyebrows and continued, as if revealing top secret information no longer made any difference, at least not to him.

"It offered a range of possibilities," he said. "Some were bizarre, such as the creation of the ideal fighting man – a remorseless killer of high skill, great courage and unquestioning obedience. The idea was to eliminate the causes of post-combat stress syndrome. But the sheer numbers involved made it totally impractical. A more workable idea was the creation of the ideal undercover agent – fearless, nerves of steel, an instinctive killer with a photographic memory, a well-honed deductive intelligence and a high threshold for pain. Or the reverse – creation of some formula that would reduce a man's mind to putty, not the old truth serum cliché, but something that would be invaluable in espionage when applied to enemy defectors or captured agents."

"And drugs were the foundation of the MK-Ultra program?"

"They were the cornerstone of many projects. We worked with mescaline, lysergic acid diethylamide, psilocybin; we had a pharmaceutical cell that also experimented with new concoctions, designer drugs, few of which offered much promise. They proved far too destructive. Drug therapy proved most effective when used in conjunction with other techniques – electrical shock, pain, fear, isolation, that sort of thing. In my own work, I used drugs along with hypnotism and achieved remarkable successes. You, for example."

"What about me?" I asked, hoping he'd at last get down to the specifics of my case. "Where do I fit into this picture?"

"If I revealed everything, Major, it could cost me my life. Excuse my reticence, but we are at the moment involved in a situation both delicate and dangerous. This much I can tell you: You were a raving madman when you were sent to me for treatment; now you are a functional human being. I could show you a film of yourself in physical restraints, a patient who alternated between wide-eyed catatonia and violent tantrums, deadly outbursts during which you were an obvious danger to yourself and anyone around you. And despite the advanced nature of your mental problems, I cured you and kept you cured for more than ten years. Even now, despite your injury, you remain functional."

"I wish I could share your pride, Ross, but most functional human beings have a past – and I don't seem to have one. If you told me how I got into this predicament, maybe I could find my own way out of it."

"It began," he said, "with a simple premise – eliminate the troubling images in your mind and implant new ones in their place. I managed to erase your former personality and create an entirely new one. You are quite literally not the same man who was wheeled into my laboratory. I'm sorry about your recent injury and the resulting amnesia. It wasn't my idea to put you in harm's way, but circumstances made it necessary. It was a gamble I had to take, even if it endangered my experiment."

"Damn it, Ross, I'm not an experiment, I'm a human being! I want to know what's behind all this – why me, why now?" I was more worried than angry, but it was the anger that resounded in my voice.

"Take it easy, Major. I don't believe the damage is irreparable. I've been able to maintain a certain balance in you for many years and I believe we can achieve that balance again. As to why this all came to the forefront just now, it's because a desperate situation arose, one that called for both your anonymity and your military expertise. We required someone without a past, someone that would pose no threat if our plan failed. We also required the reflexive behavior I had managed to sublimate in you for many years. I was convinced you still retained the instincts that had made you a hero in two wars, and now we needed those instincts. We were fighting fire with fire. Those who wanted to undermine our activities had sent a trained assassin against us – Frank Carter. I felt that you were more than his equal, that in the moment of truth, it would be you who survived."

"My God, this is incredible! You mean that you needed a killer, so you resurrected the killer instincts in me? That's not simple malpractice, Ross, that's criminal!"

"I can understand your reaction, but I could see no other course. I had confidence in you. I had created you, and felt perfectly justified in manipulating you. You performed admirably, you survived."

"Not by much, I didn't," I said. "That slug nearly took my head off. Not only that, but I'm still a target. It looks as if you're dealing with a lot of poor losers, so my survival may be only temporary. I want to know who's after me and why. Is it your fascist pal Peabody and his friends in The Group, or Felkerson and his weekend warriors in Omega Force? And if I killed Frank Carter, was it because he killed General Parks? There seems to be a connection between Parks' death, the Alaska shootout and the explosion."

"The general was a victim of the system, McCauley, not of an assassin. He was a great patriot, the founder of Omega Force. Under his command it was a proud and honorable paramilitary organization that served this nation well for years. Its activities were top secret, but trust me when I say that it performed heroically more than once and that its members were heroes, unsung heroes who will never be recognized as such by their fellow Americans. But now it's all falling apart while some of us, perhaps in vain, try to hold it together."

"By recruiting neo-Nazis? I don't think it'll work, Ross. If anything it'll give Omega Force a black eye for all time. Those people in The Group are crazies, and you of all people should know it."

"We had nowhere else to turn. We were established as creatures of the CIA, and when that connection was severed we lost our cachet with the federal government – our protection was gone, funding and supplies were cut off, a whispering campaign against us undercut our recruitment efforts through military channels. More importantly, we were discredited before Congress. The press picked up on it and suddenly we were an embarrassment to the CIA, which was already under fire for miscalculations and ill-advised intervention in foreign affairs. When Congress got tough with the agency, Omega Force was doomed. It could never withstand public scrutiny. We were doing the country's dirty work, engaging in covert activities that not only were immoral but often illegal. When the CIA cut us adrift, our regulars quit and went home. We could no longer offer them the pay or the adventure or the satisfaction of fighting for their country. A handful of us, some of whom had been with the force since its inception, decided to try to hold it together by any means possible and wait for the political climate to change. We knew the time would come again when we'd be needed. But in our weakened state, members of The Group infiltrated our ranks. Parks was furious when he found out. The Group had an ugly and well-publicized reputation around the country for redneck radicalism, racism and crime – all kinds of criminal acts from armed robbery to murder. The general was aware of it, but without the support of the CIA he was powerless to do much about it. Then he did something stupid, and I'm certain it led to his death – he went to the CIA, told them what was happening to Omega Force and pleaded for help."

Ross was shaking badly and his pallor was obvious even in the dim light of his office. He buried his head in his hands for a moment, then got up from his desk and walked to a window where the drapes were drawn. He pulled the curtain aside and stared into the dark of night as if looking beyond the present into a future he dreaded. At last he squared his shoulders and returned to his desk.

"It's not fair to blame this crisis on the general. He was old and tired and far too trusting. Some of us younger officers must share the blame. We tried our best to convince the agency that we would help him keep things under control. But by the time Parks went to Washington looking for assistance, he couldn't even find moral support. They brushed him off, told him to come back again when the political winds were blowing from a different direction. It was a terrible blow to him. He returned a broken man, but still determined to keep a small cadre of volunteers combat ready. He knew very well the nature of the men he had to work with and it sickened him. His orders were ignored; he was patronized. He had lost control and he knew it. Even before his death, members of The Group had taken command of Omega Force."

"But if the agency fails to act, that takeover is going to come back to haunt them," I said.

"I don't think so," said Ross. "I think it's part of a plan to establish plausible deniability. They will have records to show Congress that Omega Force was officially disbanded and that this upstart organization is not of their making. They may even place the blame on General Parks for allowing Omega Force to become the paramilitary arm of antigovernment fanatics. I've worked with the agency for many years and I know how ruthless it can be. I think key officials are allowing Omega Force to assist in its own destruction by ignoring The Group's takeover."

"Then why haven't you jumped ship?" I asked, suspecting now that Ross' dabbling in the cocaine trade might be a misguided effort to help support Omega Force.

"Because I felt that someone with contacts in Washington ought to keep an eye on things before they got out of hand. I happen to agree with General Parks that a covert paramilitary organization is necessary to confront the threat of communism in this hemisphere – covert operations as an alternative to overt military action that might involve the nation in an all-out war. But time is growing short. The Group is steering us toward disaster, and controlling elements in the CIA are ignoring the threat."

"Do you mean that there are other elements within the agency that support the Omega Force concept?"

"Of course there are, but at the moment they lack the political support to be effective."

"Did the CIA destroy the Parks estate?"

"I think so. I believe they did it with a mole, someone they thought we'd never suspect – one of our most trusted officers, an Omega Force veteran and a top advisor to Parks."

"Who would that be?"

He looked me square in the eye and replied with a wry grin, "Carter, of course."

"Carter! You mean you took me out of mothballs to get rid of a CIA undercover agent? I don't get it. Why go to so much trouble? Why resurrect an old has-been like me? Why go all the way to Alaska to kill him?"

"First of all, you were a valuable experiment that need to be tested in utmost secrecy. Carter was an avid hunter, so Campbell invited you both to his lodge. Your assignment was to kill Carter; his was to kill you. It was the perfect test. If you succeeded, it would dispel Campbell's doubts about you. If you failed, Campbell himself would have killed Carter and disposed of you both where you'd never be found."

"But it would have been so much simpler just to kill Carter…"

"I wanted him to test you for a key role in an upcoming Omega Force operation, but he didn't trust my work. Neither did Felkerson. You were an unknown quantity and they didn't want to gamble on you. I was confident your performance would reassure them both and I was right."

"Not quite. Carter winged me, and Felkerson isn't convinced of anything. I get the feeling his money was on Carter and he's a sore loser. I think he's the one who's been trying to kill me."

"I don't know. It's possible. He's made it clear he wants you out of the way, but Campbell's in charge, and Campbell liked what he saw."

"What about Peabody. Is he just Mr. Deep Pockets, the guy who pays the tab that the taxpayers used to pick up?"

"On the contrary, Connie's sympathetic to our cause, but he'd rather spend his money on big cars and fancy uniforms. He's a little boy playing dress-up, living a fantasy life and loving it. He offers us a forum for recruitment, nothing more. He spends only enough on the activities of his unit to keep his members honest. He can't abide the criminal tactics that other units of The Group employ. I mean, can you imagine him robbing a bank or holding up a liquor store?"

He smiled affectionately when he spoke of Peabody, which I took as a reflection of his fondness for the guy. But I also noticed Ross was looking a bit drawn, as if our long session had exhausted him. It was very late and I was reluctant to press him further on the matter that concerned me most – my military and medical files, which were nowhere in sight. But there was one thing I had to ask while he was in the mood to talk.

"You said I had a key role to play in Omega Force," I said. "What did you mean?"

"I meant there's no one left to keep a rein on Campbell, and I knew I could trust you to do that job. And it's urgent that you accept that responsibility soon, very soon."

"What's the rush?"

"Campbell's ready to conduct an operation that would be disastrous for the country if it were carried out. It could lead to war. He's obsessed, McCauley, unbalanced. He was suspicious of Carter and wanted him out of the way; I convinced him you could both get rid of Carter and also play that key role in the operation. At the same time, you'd be my man on the inside, someone who could stop Campbell, one way or another. I'd do it myself, but I'm not suited for that sort of thing."

"If Campbell's such a nut, how did he take over Omega Force?"

"He had a lot going for him. He was a decorated hero of the Vietnam War, a dedicated patriot who had served two hitches in the Marines. He came to us highly recommended by sources in Washington. None of us knew that he was a member of The Group. He took a leading role in several of our most important advisory missions to Latin America, training anticommunist guerrilla forces. General Parks rewarded him with a commission and later named him to his staff. He ingratiated himself to the old man, convinced him he could save Omega Force after the government cut us off. But the general insisted in one last effort to keep government support alive. He failed, and when he returned from Washington disillusioned and suffering from the ravages of old age, it was easy for Campbell to step in and take over."

"I'd like to know more about this operation Campbell has planned," I said. "What's so important about it that it necessitated Carter's assassination and a bombing that killed the general's family?"

"Campbell plans to involve the United States in a war by starting a brushfire that can't help but burn out of control. The CIA learned about it through Carter and probably ordered him to halt it any way he could – the agency wanted Omega Force to die on the vine, not explode in its face. Carter suspected he might be the target of the Alaska hunting trip, but probably gambled that he could kill Campbell first. But when you were thrown into the mix Carter had to hedge his bet. I think he planted the bombs at the Parks estate and timed them to go off if and when he failed to return to defuse them. That way, if he couldn't kill Campbell, at least he could destroy his arsenal and thereby send a powerful signal to Washington."

"But why didn't you try to stop it? You seem to be in tight with both sides."

"I'm not a fighter, McCauley. I'm too old and I'm not well. That's why I'm asking for your help. Go along with Campbell. He says he has a key role for you to play, and Felkerson won't bother you once you're under Campbell's wing. I know you can do it. You're a bona fide war hero, a proven patriot. You couldn't refuse this chance to serve your country."

"That's nonsense! I can refuse anything. I'm not your robot anymore. I've got a mind of my own, such as it is. I can't remember being a war hero and I'm too old to learn now. A guy can get killed playing soldier at my age. Campbell's not fool enough to gamble on me now that he knows that my brains have been rescrambled. How can he possibly put any trust in me?"

"I told you – he's seen you in action. All he needs now is assurance that you're not faking amnesia. That's why he had Felkerson tail you back to San Francisco, to see if you'd slip up somewhere along the way. You almost blew it by bumbling into Connie's meeting, but I assured Felkerson I'd check you out and give you a clean bill of health. Campbell would trust you, if you'd just put a little effort into it. Do it, Major. Do it for your country."

I didn't like the way Ross always threw in the "Major" when he was playing me for a sucker. I got up and pulled the drapes open. It was beginning to get light and the early morning commuter traffic already was getting heavy along Lombard Street. I weighed Ross' plea and decided it really didn't need an immediate response. I only had to keep him on a string for a while until I found out what I wanted to know about my past. I also wanted to find out more about Campbell's war games. Who knows? If he really was crazy enough to plunge us all into World War III, it would take more than an addle-brained retread like me to stop him. On the other hand, I didn't like the idea of neo-Nazis representing this country, in uniform or out. There was enough hate in the world without institutionalizing it. History didn't need another Hitler, and if that's how Campbell visualized himself, maybe I ought to try to do something about it. When I turned around I saw that Ross had laid his head on his arms and appeared to be asleep at his desk. I went over and shook him awake.

"Sorry," he said groggily, "I think I've picked up a virus. I've got to get home and get some rest."

"It doesn't look to me like you're in any condition to drive."

"I'll be all right. Can I give you a lift?"

"Never mind. I'd rather walk. I've got a lot to think about. Besides, I need a breath of fresh air. I'll be in touch."

Chapter 13

I did have a lot on my mind and it was a great morning for a walk. I hiked up Broderick to Union Street, through Cow Hollow and over Russian Hill where the sun broke through the fog and the sea air was fresh and crisply cool. Working people began hurrying into the street from apartment buildings and I felt sorry for them having to spend such a beautiful day in an office building. I felt even sorrier for myself – knowing I'd have to spend most of my day sleeping off a long and tiring night that was beginning to catch up with me. At the bottom of the hill North Beach already was bustling with life, but Washington Square was an emerald sea of tranquility nestling snuggly under the Gothic spires of Sts. Peter and Paul. I sprawled there on the grass near the firemen's monument for a rest before tackling the steep climb up Telegraph Hill. Watching the neighborhood residents gathering at the bus stop for the trip downtown reassured me that real people were still the majority in America, not the creeps and spooks and cold-eyed fanatics that I'd been rubbing elbows with over the past twenty-four hours. Life wasn't neo-fascist cell meetings and secret combat units and illicit experiments to screw up men's minds. Life was getting up in the morning and going to work and coming home again at night to a loving family and keeping your nose clean and your eye on the stars. And if you were fortunate enough to live that life in a city as wonderful as San Francisco, so much the better.

I soon drifted off into a deep sleep before a nightmare drove me suddenly awake again. It was another one of those horrible dreams that would have had me crawling up the walls at home, but here it sent me bolt upright in the warm mid-morning sunlight. The dream was less surrealistic than the flashbacks that haunted me recently, more lifelike and more frightening. I was on a search and destroy mission that involved a night jump, an eerie plunge into darkness with the wind hot on my face, and a jarring landing in a field of elephant grass. I unbuckled my 'chute, checked my weapons and then lay silently listening to the night sounds of the jungle. I cradled my M-16 and crawled on knees and elbows toward a clearing where I could see a small village, a dozen or so thatched huts. To my right and left I could hear the metallic clicks of automatic weapons being readied – and then mayhem! An explosion of gunfire erupted and I leaped to my feet and charged to the nearest hut. I kicked the flimsy door open and squeezed the trigger, raking the shadowy figures that cowered in the darkness. My muzzle blasts lit their faces, old people, women and children, as their screams drowned out the chatter of gunfire. It was a scene of carnage so real, so terrifying that I must have let out a cry. I awoke to find a cop standing over me.

"You okay, buddy?" he asked. "You better move on, you're scaring hell out of the kids here."

I looked around at a ring of cherubic faces surrounding me, all wide-eyed and wondering. Behind them was their day-care teacher, a woman with tired, drawn features that belied her 30-odd years. Like the cop, she looked sad but understanding, not angry or frightened.

"I'm sorry," I said. "I must have been dreaming. I'll be getting on my way, if that's okay, officer."

"No problem, buddy. There's no law against dreaming. Okay kids, let's break it up. The gentleman's fine; let's be moving along."

The young woman herded her charges toward the sidewalk, glancing back at me as she went. She seemed sympathetic, as if somehow she understood the demons that inhabited the dark corners of the mind. Maybe she had her own war casualty at home and knew there wasn't a damn thing she or anyone else could do about it. I gave her an apologetic smile and with a shrug of my shoulders trudged up Union Street and home. Kicking back in my recliner I tried not to think, just let my mind go blank, but weird visions kept creeping into my consciousness. Finally I took a page from Ross' book and flicked on the audio cassette player to let Beethoven chase the ghosts away. As I drifted off I wondered where I'd be today if it hadn't been for Ross and his crazy experiments. Or *who* I'd be. It was nearly five o'clock when the telephone rang. It was Dan Tobin.

"I've had a very busy but interesting day, McCauley. I thought you might have been trying to call."

"No, I've been asleep."

"Sorry to awaken you. I've been on the phone for hours and I've turned up some information that I'm sure will intrigue you. I think I've found the woman Pete McCauley once intended to marry – and their son."

"That's a big load, Tobin. Why don't you back off and come on a bit slower."

"I've been following the Omaha leads and called around to several high schools there. I located Peter J. McCauley's former English teacher, a very nice old lady who had taken a special interest in your elusive alter ego. He was an orphan, it seems, living in a foster home that he hated. He enlisted in the army in the summer of 1950, leaving behind a girlfriend and little else. The teacher said the girl followed McCauley to California. She gave me her name and guess what – I think I've found her."

"I'm not sure I'm ready for this, Tobin."

"McCauley was stationed at Fort Ord at the time and the girl tracked him down, hoping he'd marry her before shipping out."

"And surprise, surprise! He didn't, right?"

"Exactly. It was the classic wartime romance, according to the teacher. The girl wrote to her that McCauley wouldn't marry her because he felt doomed to die in a far off land, Korea in this case. She wanted something to remember him by, and he obliged. Voila, a son! The lovers corresponded briefly, but she never told him about her pregnancy and apparently never heard from him again."

"And nobody lived happily ever after," I guessed.

"That's an understatement. I found her living in a trailer park in San Jose. She works occasionally as a department store clerk. She's been on welfare for years. I thought we might drop around to see her this evening. It could be our first positive identification. Surely she would recognize the father of her own child, even after all these years. Don't you agree?"

It wasn't a pleasant prospect. I was pretty certain by now that I wasn't really Peter J. McCauley. On the other hand, I was. That was the only name I knew, and the only identity I had, and only God and Col. David Ross really knew where I got it. But to look into the eyes of someone who had known the real Peter J. McCauley intimately – well, that had the makings of a trauma I really didn't need. And what if turned out that I really was the guy who had for one reason or another deserted this woman thirty-five years ago?

"I don't like the idea," I concluded.

"Of course you don't. Who would? But I think it would be noble of you to see her, nevertheless. It might be uncomfortable for a moment or two, but look at the advantages. You may get first-hand evidence that you're *not* McCauley and we can drop that whole line of inquiry and try another. Also, if this woman can prove that McCauley is the father of her child, perhaps she or her son can lay claim to a $300,000 inheritance. She sounds as if she could use some financial help. And let's not overlook the possibility that she might offer some clue to your true identity. You've got everything to gain and nothing to lose."

"Unless she throws her arms around my neck and greets me as her long lost lover and the boy grabs me by the knees and calls me Daddy."

"Not likely, McCauley. The boy, as you call him, would be in his middle thirties by now. I'll be around after dinner, say at seven o'clock. And walk up to the top of the hill, will you? I don't want to get caught in that damned cul-de-sac again."

111

I was in the shower when B.J. let herself into my apartment and rapped on the bathroom door.

"Where in hell have you been, Pete? I was worried about you."

"I can't hear you. Wait until I rinse off."

"Sure, I'll get your towel."

"Just hand it to me. I haven't got time for fun and games."

"Got a hot date?"

"Yeah. Maybe with my son and his mother."

"What's that supposed to mean? And where were you last night?"

"It's a long story. Actually it's two long stories, and I don't have time for either of them. How about scrambling some eggs? We'll have a bite to eat. I've got an appointment at seven and I'm famished. Run along now and whip up something while I get dressed."

"God, you're demanding, McCauley. I don't know why I put with this shit."

"Be a good girl, and stir up a martini first. I need a jolt."

The fact was I'd much rather have spent the evening with B.J., but duty called. She promised to be waiting when I came home, and that kept me focused on what was to be a short but difficult evening. We lumbered down the Bayshore Freeway with Tobin's aging Olds spewing huge clouds of black exhaust. We didn't talk much. He could tell I was nervous, and when he did speak at last as we pulled into a run-down trailer park it was an attempt to put me at ease.

"She knows nothing about you, McCauley. I've told her very little, only that I'm trying to find the legal heirs to an estate. I won't introduce you at first. We'll let her size you up to see if there's a glimmer of recognition. My bet is there won't be. Just act natural. You're a friend accompanying me to a business meeting, nothing more. If there is no reaction, I may ask her if she recognizes you. If not, that's it. Help me find 103."

Most of the lot numbers were missing or obscured by overgrowths of ivy. The park was a mess with all manner of debris littering the cramped little front yards. The people who were out of their tin boxes were uniformly old and colorless and weary looking, as if it had taken a lifetime of hard labor to get precisely nowhere and they had been drained and exhausted by the struggle. The women looked lonely and resigned, the way women probably have looked throughout history after trusting their men to provide for them in old age and realizing too late they had failed. The men, and there weren't many to be seen, looked angry and defiant and wasted by lives of drudgery. What a miserable way to go out, I thought. What a rotten way to culminate a life. I wondered how the woman would look. When we found 103 it proved to be the exception in this crowded slum. It was well kept up, with fresh plants in the tiny window boxes, its walkway swept clean. A rocking chair sat invitingly on the tiny front porch and a small garden lamp lit the path to her door. She appeared there before Tobin had squeezed out from behind the wheel. I was already out of the car and she greeted me politely as she came down the steps.

"No," I said, pointing. "That's Mr. Tobin. I'm just a friend along for the ride."

She looked little better than the other women we'd seen in the park, older than her fifty-plus years. Her hair was streaked with gray, there were bags under her eyes and the skin of her neck was sagging and wrinkled. She was wearing a cheap cotton dress, but it was so clean I could smell the freshness of it as she stepped past me to greet Tobin.

"I've just finished the dinner dishes, Mr. Tobin," she said. "I was about to pour a cup of coffee. Won't you and your friend join me?"

"Thank you, Ms. Carey," he said. "But I think we should not impose on your hospitality. I only hope we are not keeping you from more important matters."

She led us into her neat, if under-furnished, living room. It was much like the trailer and the woman herself, aging but clean and neat. She directed us to a couch covered with a handsome Afghan and took a chair facing us across a bare coffee table that had been polished until it glistened.

"I'm here on the behalf of the estate of a Nebraska farmer named Lundgren, Ms. Carey. Does that name mean anything to you?"

She thought for a moment, her eyes flitting about the room as if searching through a musty old storehouse of memories.

"It sounds vaguely familiar, but I suppose there are a lot of Lundgrens in Nebraska. It's my native state, but I can't honestly say I know anyone by that name."

"I see," Tobin said pensively. "The reason I ask is because the executors of the Lundgren estate have asked me to locate one Peter J. McCauley or his heirs. I have reason to believe that you once were acquainted with Mr. McCauley, were you not?"

She reacted to that name as if someone had slapped her face. Then her shoulders sagged under some invisible burden and tears welled in her eyes.

"I knew Mr. McCauley many years ago, Mr. Tobin," she said softly. "We were, how should I say it – we were high school sweethearts. But I've neither seen nor heard from him for more than thirty years. What possible connection could this have with me?"

"You were never married to Mr. McCauley?"

"No. We were never married." Her voice was small and forlorn.

"We have been unable to locate Mr. McCauley," Tobin went on. "We suspect he may no longer be with us. If that is indeed the case, then we must look further, perhaps for Mr. McCauley's heirs. This is the reason I must ask such personal questions. I'm sure you understand."

Ms. Carey sat erect and squared her shoulders. Her cheeks were red and her eyes alive with resentment.

114

"I think I know what you're getting at, Mr. Tobin. I can't imagine how you could know such a thing, but you must be referring to my son."

"Could he be..."

"Could he be Peter McCauley's child? I'm not prepared to answer that question before strangers, nor can I think of any reason why I should," she said defiantly.

"There is one very good reason, Ms. Carey – $300,000. A tidy sum, don't you agree? Certainly reason enough to answer the question, no matter how embarrassing."

"Some things in life have no price, Mr. Tobin. I value my privacy perhaps even more than $300,000."

"But would your son feel the same way? That is the question you must ask yourself. The inheritance may be legally his, and we can only get to him through you. Would you stand between your son and such a sum? Won't you help us locate him?"

"No, I would not stand in his way, and as for locating him, that's easy. He's in the kitchen."

She stood up, visibly upset, and led us into her kitchen. There at a Formica-topped table sat a man of indeterminate years, staring at the tabletop. It was apparent at a glance that he suffered from Down's syndrome. He did not look up when we entered. Ms. Carey went to his side and gently put her arm around his shoulder, leaning close and looking into his face.

"Johnny, how are you feeling? Are you happy?" she asked.

He looked up slowly, the light of recognition dawning unevenly in his eyes. Then just as slowly a smile crossed his puffy, pallid face with its stubble of beard. His mother smoothed his hair lovingly and looked at us.

"This is my son, John. That was Peter's middle name, you know. Peter John McCauley. I never told Peter about his son – never. The Lundgren you mentioned might have been Peter's granduncle. As I recall he owned a farm west of town. Peter mentioned him occasionally. I think he may have gone to visit him once. That's really all I know about him. I doubt that he would want his fortune to go to Peter's illegitimate child, particularly not to a retarded son," she said bitterly.

"I'm afraid it's no longer within Mr. Lundgren's power to influence the disposition of his estate, Ms. Carey. The law must do that now. I believe your son might have a legal claim, if you're prepared to swear to his parentage in a court of law."

I could almost see the wheels going around in her head. She had suffered long and hard with her burden and the prospect of an inheritance was obviously something she could not afford to reject out of hand.

"You don't have to answer now, Ms. Carey," Tobin said. "I'm only a private investigator. I have no say in the matter, one way or the other. But I would like to tell the executors, a law firm in Omaha, that I have located Mr. McCauley's natural son. Will you permit me to do that?"

"It might mean help for Johnny," she said quietly. "It might mean he won't be alone, if I should…"

"It might indeed. I'll convey that word to the executors, then. Oh, one more thing. Have you ever been married to anyone, Ms. Carey? It could have a bearing on this case."

"No," she said with a thin little smile that failed to hide the pain the question caused her. "Carey is my family name. One man was interested once, until he met Johnny."

"I think I understand, Ms. Carey. And finally, in order to establish our objectivity, I must ask you if you have ever seen me or my associate before."

She looked surprised, but dutifully studied us both carefully before responding, as if a wrong answer might somehow jeopardize her son's prospects. She was particularly careful in scrutinizing my face, since she hadn't really looked at me carefully until now.

"No," she concluded. "I have never seen either one of you before in my life."

116

"Thank you, Ms. Carey. I'll be in touch with you, probably within the month, I should think."

"Good night, Mr. Tobin. Good night, Mr....":

"Harrison," I lied. "My name is Harrison."

Chapter 14

I was now more certain than ever that only Ross could answer the questions that were uppermost in my mind: Who am I, and how and why did I become Peter J. McCauley? And who was trying to kill me? Tobin let me out at the intersection of Union and Montgomery and I walked down to Calhoun Terrace and my apartment. It was only ten o'clock and B.J. was waiting just as she said she'd be. She'd gone back to her own apartment during my absence to shower and change clothes and she looked fresh and sweet enough to eat. I made the mistake of telling her so.

"You're kinky, Pete," she gushed, "and I love it. But first you owe me an explanation. Where were you tonight and last night, and what are you up to anyway."

"I'm still looking for answers, sweetheart, and I'm not getting many. What I know for certain is that I'm not Peter J. McCauley. I sat face to face with his former lover tonight and I was a complete stranger to her. I also know that there *was* a McCauley once and for some reason Ross has given me his identity. I've got a fair idea now who McCauley was, but not who I was before Ross made me a guinea pig in one of his experiments. I'd also like to know why Ross has worked for years to convince me that I am who I'm really not."

"Run that by me again, Pete. You lost me somewhere."

"I didn't lose you, B.J., I lost me. And I'm going to find out who I really am, if I have to beat it out of Ross. He's playing coy with me, holding my identity for ransom so I'll play war games with him. Frankly, I'm too old to play soldier. It's dangerous. And if I'm going to put my life on the line, I want it to be my life, not Peter J. McCauley's."

"I've always liked you just as you are, Pete," she said, making herself comfortable next to me on the couch. "I like you a lot, but I don't want to get involved in your weird identity crisis. I know who you are. You're my lover and there's nothing I like better than making love with you.

118

That's what I want to do right now. And when we're through I want you to take me out for a late supper and then I want to do it again, someplace neat – maybe on a BART train while it's zooming under the bay. Or up on that cold wall at Coit Tower with the whole city spread out before us. Remember that time?"

"B.J., you're an absolute nut."

"There are no absolutes. I learned that in Philosophy 101 at State. Everything is relative, and right now it's Friday night and I'm relatively horny, so let's get it on."

She kicked off her shoes, turned off the lamp and went over to put on some music. It was a jazz instrumental, slow and dreamy, a tape she'd brought along for just this purpose. It was smooth, compelling, with a soft, insistent beat. She began to dance there in the dim light that filtered through the blinds, slithering out of her dress in an entrancing strip tease reminiscent of Rita Hayworth's dance scene in "Gilda." It crossed my mind that this kid wasn't even born when Rita "put the blame on Mame, boy." But how can a guy feel guilty when B.J. was doing her best to turn him on? She had a firm young body that needed no support garments, and tonight she wasn't wearing any. She was lithe and beautiful and so eager that her eyes fairly glowed in the semi-darkness. She paused to unsnap her garter belt and peeled off her stockings with the grace of a veteran Burlesque dancer, slowly so my eyes would have time to drink in every curve as she posed there in nothing but her little girl grin. Then she picked up the beat of the music again, resuming her special show for Daddy.

It was dance night in Fantasy Ballroom as she twisted and twirled, rising to the beat and bending low again with incredible grace and beauty. At first her eyes would catch mine with each turn as she spun closer to me, tempting me to reach out for her. But then suddenly I realized I had become an anonymous spectator, an unseen face in the darkness beyond the footlights at this bizarre performance. She had pirouetted her way into her private sexual limbo, separated

119

from reality, lost in deep longings and seeking desperately for the release that only the ultimate ecstasy could bring her. My impulse was to resist her, to snap her out of it somehow. But she was irresistible. I was ready for her when she fell upon me at last and joined willing in her pagan ritual, writhing in time with the music, laboring ever faster as the beat quickened. She uttered a little cry as the music reached a crescendo. I watched her face in the dim light, saw her eyes staring blankly into empty space, never meeting mine. She had lost any desire to please me, so completely submerged was she in her quest for gratification. At last she fell back exhausted and detached and lay there breathing heavily while the tape spun on, filling the shadowy room with mellow music that lulled her to sleep.

I slipped out of her grasp and got up to look out over the bay. I felt as if my insides had been pulled out, leaving me empty and unsatisfied. It was a curious sensation that gave me the feeling I was little more than an object to fulfill her wild desires. I began to think about B.J.'s mad passions and how different it had been with Cindy Albright that night aboard the Stardancer. They were both beautiful women and wonderful lover-makers, but to B.J. I didn't exist. I was the right age for her peculiar tastes, I had the requisite plumbing, and I was handy. Beyond that I was nothing to her, a surrogate for a father with whom she was obsessed. I was frankly tired of being a non-person, an object she used to feed her demons when she was lost in her psychotic quest. I wondered if her hang-ups would ever permit her to love anyone, wondered what her father would think of her now, wondered if he knew just what a screwed up little girl he'd left behind him. Even as she lay there all warm and soft and desirable, I made up my mind to dump her. I didn't want to be her therapist. Whatever I had been before I got that bump on my noggin, I wanted to be my own man again. I wanted a real woman, a woman like Cindy. I wanted someone I could talk to, adult conversation, adult emotions, adult responses. I wanted to get my own head straightened out and begin living my life with the lights on, eyeball to eyeball.

B.J. woke up hungry, slipped into my robe and came into the kitchen where I was making coffee.

"I thought you were going to take me out to dinner last night."

"How about some scrambled eggs, toast and coffee?"

"Cheap bastard."

"Don't blame me! You were the one who passed out."

"You took advantage of me."

"You're goofy. Go in and get cleaned up. After breakfast I'll let you take me on some errands."

"I can't. I've got some shopping to do."

"Okay, so I'll drop you off downtown and meet you later for dinner. I do owe you a dinner."

* * *

It was noon when I dropped her off and told her I'd meet her back at the apartment later. Then I headed out to Letterman. I got nothing but a suspicious stare from the guard on duty. He said he'd never heard of Doctor Ross. He said the office I inquired about was empty and he couldn't let me in without notifying the duty officer. I showed him my military ID and he unlocked the door and went off to telephone the sergeant of the guard. Ross' office wasn't just empty, it had been stripped. There was a small white rectangle on the wall behind his desk where his medical license had been. His desk drawers were empty, as were the filing cabinets where he'd kept his records. I hurried out and caught the guard just as he began dialing.

"Forget it, Corporal. I got the wrong information. Thanks anyway."

I was pondering where to turn next and decided to give Kohler a call. I didn't want him to give up on me, because I had a hunch I'd need him before long.

"No," I told him, "I haven't got anything solid yet. After I touch a few bases I'll fill you in on what I've learned...Yeah, I think I know where the stuff is coming

121

from, but Ross may not be our man. You said you wanted to go to the top...No, I won't take any chances, believe me. No heroics, unless you're backing me up...Yes, I'll call. But right now Ross has given me the slip and I've got to catch up with him... I haven't the foggiest, but his wife will know. I'm going to call on her next. Right, he's probably at home. I'll be in touch."

The Rosses lived in a spacious ranch-style home on a winding street in one of the San Francisco Peninsula's nicer neighborhoods – not pretentious, but nice, with well-tended landscaping and enough of it to keep the house set apart from the next door residences. It was separated from the quiet street by a broad expanse of lawn rimmed by flower gardens. Mrs. Ross herself came to the door. She was a small woman, about sixty, I guessed, with a trim figure and tanned skin that suggested she was a regular on the golf course. Her hair was white and close cropped. Her nose was just a bit too large to call her a beauty, but she was undeniably attractive and youthful looking. She didn't fit the description Tobin gave me of a bored suburban housewife who had taken a job as a bank teller. When I asked to see her husband she stiffened and asked me why.

"I'm an old friend. I got no answer at his office and since I was passing by..."

"I'm sorry," she said brusquely. "I don't know where he is. It's the lunch hour, have you tried his club?"

"No, I haven't." She was nervous, her eyes jumping all over, looking beyond me as if I might have accomplices hiding in her shrubbery. I tried to put her at ease. "I guess I could telephone later. When do you expect him home?"

It was really none of my business when she expected him home, but she apparently had made up her mind that I wasn't going to leave her alone, so she may as well come clean.

"Doctor Ross no longer makes his home here," she said. "If he calls, whom shall I say was trying to reach him?"

"Harrison," I said. "My name is Harrison. I knew the doctor years ago in the Army. He said if I ever got to San Francisco I should look him up, but he wasn't at his office. I don't get around this way often, so I thought you might…"

"Doctor Ross and I are separated," she said. "I don't know where he is. He does call occasionally, if you want to give me your number."

"That won't be necessary. I'll drop him a line at Letterman. He may not even remember me. Thanks, Mrs. Ross."

I could feel her eyes on me as I went down the walk to the street. I didn't hear the door close until I was nearly out of sight. When I got back behind the wheel of B.J.'s Bug, I knew where to look next: The Opera Plaza apartment of Conrad Peabody III. I wondered if that was why she was so nervous. Maybe she suspected I was a CIA operative who'd found out Ross was a closet homosexual, or dabbling in dope. I didn't care what she thought. I had to find Ross and get my files. I was through playing games with him.

Before driving back to the city I took a swing by the First Church of Christ Militant, where Tobin said the Rosses attended services. It was a fairly new building and it looked out of place among the large old homes in the neighborhood. One of those old homes stood close by the parish hall and I took it to be the rectory. The only thing that set the church apart from others was its somewhat ostentatious display of the American Flag from a tall pole in the front lawn. The placard at the foot of the flagpole made it certain that I'd be dropping in first thing Sunday morning. It listed the times of the services and the name of the pastor – the Rev. Robert Campbell.

When I got home I gave Tobin a call, just for insurance and to see if he had turned up anything new. He answered on the first ring.

"McCauley, Dan. I just wanted to tell you I've checked out a couple of your leads on Ross. He's got an attractive wife. They're split…No, just separated, have been for a

123

while, she says. Ross keeps his slippers under someone else's bed these days, and I think I know whose...No, she seemed scared. I think she knows about his extracurricular activities and is afraid the CIA will find out...Protective? Maybe, but more likely to shield the daughter. I'm not sure, but I also got a line on Campbell. He runs the church where you said the Rosses attended services...Yes, I plan to drop in on his sermon Sunday morning, if my presence doesn't bring down a thunderbolt...Who knows? I might even get religion. Anyway, I plan to drop in on Peabody at his apartment in the Opera Plaza...Right; I might need a backup. Peabody can be a nasty little creep, and if Ross is there...Yes, let's say that if I don't call you by four this afternoon, you drop around Peabody's place to see that I'm okay...Yes, I'm driving a light blue Beetle, 1974. I'll park it in the basement garage...It may not be necessary at all, just a precaution. Security's pretty slack there. Just tell 'em you're serving a summons or something...Right. And remember, if you don't hear from me by four, come arunnin'."

Chapter 15

I got past the security guard at the Opera Plaza by falling in with a group of residents returning from a shopping trip. I followed them aboard the elevator as if I belonged there and rode to the top floor. I really didn't know what to expect when I knocked on Connie Peabody's door, but it certainly wasn't the raving maniac who answered. He didn't peek cautiously from behind the latch chain as he had on my first visit, but flung the door wide as if he were going to attack anyone who might be standing there. He stood glaring at me with sweat running down his brow and dripping off his pudgy cheeks. His face was red and so were his eyes, as if he had been crying.

"What in hell do *you* want?" he stormed.

Given his obvious anger I figured his next move would be to slam the door in my face, so I stiff-armed him and barged into the apartment before he had time to resist. That didn't improve his disposition.

"GET OUT!" he screamed. "Get out of here before I call the police!"

"Take it easy, Peabody. I'm looking for Ross and I think you know where he is."

He slammed the door shut and came at me menacingly, stopping with his florid face only inches from mine.

"I don't know where he is," he hissed through clenched teeth. "He may be roasting in hell for all I care. But I'll tell you one thing, he's never coming back here again, never!"

"What's the matter, has your boyfriend walked out on you?"

"Not that it's any of your damned business, but the fact is I threw him out. He's a cheating son-of-a-bitch, and wherever he is I hope he drops dead. And if you're one of his friends, I hope you drop dead, too. Now get out of here, or

I'll call the police and have you arrested, so help me God I will."

"Ross has cleared out of Letterman, his private office hasn't heard from him and he's not at home. That leaves you, Peabody. I figure he's here, or that you know where he is. If he's skipped out, he might have left some things here, probably several boxes. He may have dumped them to lighten his load. Now are you going to tell me where they are, or am I going to have to beat it out of you?"

I tried to sound menacing, but it was difficult to play the tough guy around a wimp like this. I tried to look flinty-eyed, but I wasn't fooling anyone, certainly not the furious Conrad Peabody III.

"Listen, cowboy, I do the beating around here, not you," he said, rising on his toes to give himself some added stature. "And if Ross walked in that door this instant I'd beat him within an inch of his life, do you understand? I'm sorry I didn't do it long ago. But he's paying for his indiscretions, and if you know what's good for you, you'll get out of here before I make you pay, too. I know what you're after, and believe me there are no drugs here – no cocaine, no heroin, nothing. I don't permit it. If he cleaned out his stash at Letterman, then he took it somewhere else, or maybe he ditched it in the woods at The Presidio. I really don't know and I don't care. I have nothing to do with drugs. It's not my style. I never allowed David to bring anything like that home with him. He brought home trouble enough as it is. If he walked through that door now, I'd kill him. So help me God, I'd kill him."

He was insanely angry, crying and shaking, ready to explode. I didn't want to be the target of his wrath. He was a stocky guy, and despite his odd inclinations in other respects, he looked as if he could be dangerous when riled. I did my best to cool him off.

"I'm not looking for drugs, Peabody, and I don't mean any harm to you or Ross. I'm looking for medical records he took from Letterman. They probably were in storage boxes, or maybe a suitcase. Did he bring anything like that here? It's my own records I want, no one else's, and I'm going to get them if I have to turn this place upside down."

Exhausted by his fury, Peabody collapsed onto his couch, his head in his hands.

"I don't know what he might have brought here," he said dejectedly. "Look around, if you insist."

He was quiet for a moment and while he collected himself I took him at his word and began to look around the apartment. It quite a showplace, what one might expect of an importer of art objects who had more money than he knew what to do with. The living room was a veritable museum. The only thing more spectacular than the décor was the view. One entire wall of glass overlooked much of the city, the bay and the hills beyond. The panorama made even his paintings look insignificant – the Picassos, the Chagalls, the Van Goghs, the Manets and the Utrillos. But when it came to sculptors Peabody found his favorite in North Beach. He displayed a half dozen pieces of Benny Bufano's work. The dining room and kitchen were huge, but the master bedroom was of more modest size, dominated by a king-size waterbed covered with a red velvet throw under a mirrored ceiling. The bath was Roman decadent, with sunken tub and gold fixtures against jet-black tile and fully mirrored walls. I wondered whether Peabody ever got tired of looking at himself. The den seemed strictly for business, done entirely in antiques, from the roll-top desk to the wired gas lamps with polished brass bases and fine cut glass globes. I was heading for the closet when I felt the cold muzzle of a gun against the back of my head.

"You've missed the best room of all," Peabody said calmly. He appeared to be in complete control of himself now; the gun he held on me was steady as a rock.

"No need for the weapon, Peabody. I'm not armed."

"I'm not surprised, since you've been a complete fool in every other respect. However, I find great comfort in this revolver, so I'll keep it, if you don't mind, while I show you my playroom."

He nudged me into the hall to the last door where we paused while he slipped a key into the lock and opened it. As I stepped into the darkness he flipped on the lights and locked the door behind us. His playroom looked like a medieval dungeon from a B movie, a torture chamber complete with a rack, a chain and handcuffs suspended from the ceiling, an assortment of whips and lashes adorning the walls and even an electric prod. In the center of the room was a piece of leather-covered furniture, a sort of kneeling bench with arm and leg clamps. It didn't take much imagination to figure out what it was for. I knew I wasn't going to like playing games with Connie Peabody, no matter which end of the whip he preferred. I found myself wondering perversely whether Ross was the whipper or the whippee. Or maybe they took turns.

"Well, I don't see anything here that looks like medical records," I said, trying to sound nonchalant, as if everyone had a sadomasochistic game room in his apartment. "How about closets, you got closets?"

He had taken off his tie with one hand while holding the gun on me with the other. It was a short-barreled revolver, a thirty-eight, and it was pointed at my groin.

"We're going to have some fun, McCauley, and when we're through you're either going to be a convert, begging me to beat you more, or you're going to be a dead man destined to go piece by piece down the garbage chute to the incinerator. Now, take your clothes off slowly."

"Wait a minute, Peabody, I don't want to be your playmate. Besides, I've got a partner downstairs who'll come storming in here with the cops if I don't show up soon."

"You're a liar, McCauley. Felkerson told me all about you. You're a loner with scrambled brains. You haven't got a friend in the world. No one's going to miss you, if you never see the light of day again. You're one of David's zombies and you're expendable. That's how he puts it, expendable. And I choose to expend you for my own pleasure. Now take off your clothes, damn it, or I'll start picking you apart with bullets."

I was wearing a windbreaker and I unzipped it slowly, looking straight into his beady little eyes, speaking quietly to keep his attention fixed.

"You really don't want an old man like me, Peabody. You want some nice young stud off the streets of the Castro, that's what you ought to have. I'm all worn out, over the hill. You know what I mean? You won't have much fun playing with me, unless you get your jollies out of seeing skinny old men die."

He was practically salivating, watching me slip slowly out of my jacket. It made me sick to think that the longer I stretched out this obscene striptease, the longer I might live. I held the jacket out to one side and shrugged, as if to ask him where to toss it.

"Just drop it on the floor," he said, nodding. That nod was the split second of inattention I needed to make my move. I whipped the jacket over his gun hand and lunged at him with all the force I could muster. He collapsed like the cream puff he was and as he fell to the floor the gun went off. I could feel the sting as the bullet grazed my leg. He went limp and I was sure he'd fainted, so I eased the revolver from his grip and loomed over him. He made a disgusting picture sprawled there on the floor and I had a strong urge to put a bullet in him.

"Get up, you creep," I spat at him. "Get up before I indulge myself and blow you to hell." When he didn't move I bent over and pried one of his eyes open. He was out cold. I slipped the revolver into my belt, dragged him over to the leather kneeling bench and strapped him face down. He was coming around now, moaning and shaking his head.

"It's a good thing this is a sound proof room, Peabody. After I leave you can yell your head off and nobody will hear you. I ought to belt you, you sick bastard, but I'm afraid you might enjoy it. Hope you're comfortable and not afraid of the dark."

I flicked off the lights, locked the door on him and returned to the den closet. There on the floor were several cardboard storage boxes stuffed with files. I rummaged through them and found a fat one marked "McCauley." I tucked it under my arm and headed for the elevator. It was three-thirty, so I stopped at a pay phone in the Opera Plaza arcade and called Tobin.

"All clear," I told him. "I've got the medical records I was looking for. Now I'll have to find a safe place for them...No, not in the car. I may not be the only one interested in the CIA's MK-Ultra program. I'm going to hide them until I can take time for some research...Peabody? He's locked in his penthouse playroom and probably madder than a wet hen...Sure, I'll be in touch."

Then I put in a call to Kohler.

"I had a run-in with Ross' boyfriend and got the files I wanted, but Ross wasn't there. I'll attend to him later...What? You must be kidding. On second thought, I guess it figures. I'd better get right over there...Hell, no, I'm not afraid. I've got to talk to him no matter what."

I stashed the McCauley files under the bonnet of B.J.'s Bug and thought about how Ross looked at our last meeting in his office. He was pale, sickly and weak; now I understood why. Kohler's men had located him through regular police channels. He'd admitted himself as a patient at San Francisco General earlier that day and sure enough, that's where I found him – in the AIDS ward.

He looked a lot worse than he had in the dim light of his office. Maybe it was the white of the sheets and the walls, but he seemed deathly pale and so weak it was all he could do to turn his head my way as I entered the room. He gave me a sardonic grin and I found myself feeling sorry for him and wondering why. He was everything I detested. He had abused his profession. He had abused the uniform of the United States Army. He had abused his humanity and even his sex. I hated his guts, but he was a man with an incurable disease and I felt sorry for him. He was going to die and there wasn't anything on God's green earth that anyone could do for him. I got right to the point.

"I still want some answers, Ross. And you're in no position now to bargain."

"You won't do it, then?" he asked.

"Play soldier? Yeah, I might. You touched a nerve, I'll admit. I'm not anxious for those nuts to get the country involved in a war. But if I do, I'll do it on my own terms and for my own reasons. And I'll do it only if I get the answers I want."

"I've told you almost everything."

"You left out some very important parts, Ross. I want to know who I was before you gave me Pete McCauley's identity. And I want to know why you chose McCauley and what happened to him."

"My records will tell you everything you want to know. I'll tell you where you can find them, if you'll promise to go along with Felkerson and Campbell. Tell them you'll do whatever they want you to do. And stick close to Felkerson. There's still hope he'll come to his senses."

I figured it would be counter-productive to tell Ross I already had his records, so I decided to keep pumping him.

"What's Felkerson's role in the operation?" I asked.

"Second in command, but more important, he's CIA, retired. He's the last credible link between Omega Force and the feds, now that I'm out of the picture."

"I thought you told me the CIA had washed its hands of Omega Force?"

"Officially, it has. But there's still a nucleus of support behind the scenes. Felkerson has friends. There are some within the establishment who understand the importance of stopping the spread of communism, and who know that direct confrontation is the only way to go about it. Felkerson could still tap into that resource, but not overtly. If the top echelon knew what he's doing, they'd eliminate him."

"How, by canceling his retirement pay?" I asked facetiously. "He plays rough. Why do you think he'd ever trust me?"

"First, because Campbell trusts you. Second, because he knows what you once could do. You were his man, McCauley. You two go way back, back to covert operations in Vietnam. But you don't remember it. I programmed it out of you years ago. Felkerson remembers, though. He was a great admirer of yours, and if you can gain his trust again you might be able to turn him around."

"He's got a strange way showing his admiration. I still think he's the one who's been trying to bump me off. And what if he's convinced your neat little package is coming undone? What if he knows I'm no longer your pet zombie? He's already suspicious. We might have been wartime buddies, but since that night at Peabody's warehouse I'm convinced he's the enemy – and I want more answers before I go after him."

"All right, I'll tell you what you won't find in the medical records. You've been part of the CIA's version of a witness protection program. The usual method was to establish a new identity for an individual – give him a new name, change his appearance, perhaps by cosmetic surgery, establish a phony background for him, all well documented. MK-Ultra went one big step beyond that. We dug into a patient's psyche, rooted out his old identity and implanted a new one, not to hide him from others, but to hide him from himself. It was quite effective and eliminated the danger that the subject would ever pose a threat. He couldn't change his mind once we had changed it for him. We created an entirely different human being."

"What had I done that made it necessary?"

"You were an accomplished killer who developed a conscience at an awkward moment in history. There was some question, even among those who greatly admired you, whether you ought to survive at all. A lot of people would be more comfortable with you dead. But you also had a

132

powerful friend who insisted that you must survive, even if meant surviving as a different person. That's why you became Peter J. McCauley."

"And what happened to McCauley? I presume he didn't have a powerful friend."

"He's dead, but his death wasn't intentional. He suffered a bad reaction of LSD and drowned in a swimming pool while undergoing treatment. I'll never know whether he committed suicide or if my procedures were simply inadequate. But his death was timely. It helped turn a failed experiment into a successful one."

"He proved to be of more value to you dead than alive?"

"Exactly. He died about the same time I was trying to invent a new identity for you. He was a natural. He had no family – no parents, no wife and no children. Ironically, he even came from your hometown. His background was perfect for the recreated you. Since I'd already erased your past, you were a clean slate. We made you into McCauley."

"And I suspect you buried him under my name."

"I could take you to his grave – your grave. Your Army records indicate you died while under treatment for mental disorders attributable to the stress of combat in Vietnam. You got a hero's burial."

"And now I'm dead and gone forever."

"Even your fingerprints were erased from federal computers. The original you has ceased to exist and rests peacefully today in Golden Gate National Cemetery."

"Which left me free to do the dirty work for Omega Force under his name," I observed. "If I'm killed or captured, the government could deny I exist. I'd be the perfect spy or the perfect assassin."

"Or the perfect hero, McCauley. You could come out of this a hero."

"Bullshit, Ross! If I'm going to die for my country, I'm going to die under my own name, not McCauley's. That's the key question now – what's my real name, who was I

133

before you started playing God? I won't make a commitment until you tell me."

"I think you will. You have no choice – no action, no answers." He reached over and buzzed for the nurse. "Visiting hours are over, McCauley."

Chapter 16

I parked B.J.'s Volkswagen on Union Street near my rented garage and hurried down the steps to her apartment. It was after five and I'd promised to take her to dinner. It was time I had a talk with her and the kind of talk I had in mind was best held after dinner. It wasn't going to improve her appetite.

"Elegant," she said. "I want to go someplace elegant."

That surprised me because she was dressed in a bizarre outfit that made her look more like a boy than a girl.

"They may make you put on a tie," I warned her.

"Not me, McCauley, you. That's the best thing about women's lib: I can wear anything I damn well please and they wouldn't dare keep me out. Besides, this is considered high fashion, and if they don't want a picket line in front of their door, they'd better let me in."

"I don't know if I have a tie," I observed.

"You have a lot of ties. Would you like a drink here before we go?"

"Thanks. I'll go down and change and be right up."

I was heading for the door when she called out: "They're in your walk-in closet on a rack way in the rear."

I took her to the Garden Court. I liked it there. The Palace Hotel had the look and smell of history and none of the young rich came there anymore. It wasn't "in" and that was fine with me. It wasn't B.J.'s idea of elegance, but what did she know? She wasn't very talkative during dinner, but over a B and B and coffee she opened up.

"I'm pretty tired of this thing of yours, Pete. It's like an obsession. You know what I mean?"

"I know it is, but I counted on your understanding."

"Well, I don't understand. No, I think I do understand, but I'm tired of understanding. Follow me?"

I could never figure her out. I'd planned to talk to her like a Dutch uncle and she had turned the tables on me. I let her ramble, on the theory that she couldn't get sore at me for what she said.

"I mean we used to have a lot of fun, and now you're always chasing around after God knows what. You're preoccupied, you know? I can't get close to you. For instance, you haven't even mentioned where you were today. Where were you today?"

"I had a run in with a sadomasochistic homosexual who pulled a gun on me. I wrestled it away from him and left him strapped on a screwing couch. Then I burglarized his apartment and went to visit his roommate in an AIDS ward."

"See what I mean? I ask a simple question and you lie to me."

"You're right about one thing, B.J. We don't communicate very well. We've got a generation gap. Maybe we ought to cool it. You shouldn't be here with me. You should be out with some nice young stud who'd hold your hand and talk about the moon in June and a happy honeymoon. How do you ever expect to latch onto a guy like that when you spend all your time with an old fart like me?"

"This is a brush-off, isn't it, Pete?" she asked. "I know one when I hear one."

"No brush-off intended. After all, you brought up the subject. And you're right. We don't communicate very well. But we'll still be neighbors, we'll still be pals. That'll never change. But..."

"But?"

"But when you're thirty-five I'll be in a rest home. Think about it. Even now people take us for father and daughter. You're a bright and charming girl. You deserve better than I can ever give you. You've got a thing in your head that tells you that you need me, but you really don't. You need a young man, someone who will take you where the action is without falling asleep in his soup. You need

136

someone whose head is screwed on straight, and you're not going to find him so long as I'm in the picture."

"Let's go home, Pete. I'll show you how much I need you."

"No! That's the problem. There's more to life than making love, no matter how many wonderful ways you can think to do it. The world's still out there when the sun comes up and you should be taking part in it."

Her lower lip was quivering now, her eyes brimming with tears. I hated to hurt her, hated it more than anything I could think of, but it had to be done, for my sake and hers. My impulse was to reach out and take her hand to comfort her, but I wouldn't let myself do it. A little show of sympathy and we'd be right back where we started.

"Just take me home," she said, sucking air to stifle her crying. "Take me home before I make a complete fool of myself."

I tried to talk to her, but everything I said sounded phony even to me, and for the most part it was the straight stuff. I told her I had some dangerous things I had to do, things that might take me away for weeks, maybe even months. There was even a chance I wouldn't be coming back. I told her all that but she just looked straight ahead, tears rolling down her cheeks, making me hate myself. I found a parking place at Union and Montgomery and walked her down the eighty-eight steps, still pleading my case and getting nowhere. I thought about all the misery she'd been through in her short life and hated myself for adding to it. She put her key in the lock and wasn't going to turn around until I grabbed her.

"Let's not leave it like this," I said. "We've still got a lot to give each other." She was a mess in the glow of her porch light, her mascara running down her cheeks with her tears, her eyes swollen. My impulse was to take her in my arms to comfort her, to tell her that tomorrow she'll have forgotten all about me. But I didn't dare. That was how it all began with her, just like that, trying to comfort her as a father might

137

do, and I knew I had to stand my ground and hang tough. She stopped crying and let her anger take over.

"Yeah, McCauley, we had a lot to give one another. Think about that next time you're out of your gourd, crawling up the walls, ranting and raving. Think about that next time you pass out on the street and there's no one there to help you home. Think about that the next time you land in jail and there's no one to bail you out. We've got a lot to give each other, but I'll be damned if I'll give you the time of day. You can go to hell!"

She jerked out of my grip and slammed the door in my face. I realized then how deeply I had hurt her. Inflicting psychological pain is so easy, especially when you do it to someone who has known so much pain already. I tried to tell myself it was for her own good but that didn't help. I hated myself for treating her so badly but there was still one more bond to sever. I went back to her VW and removed the McCauley file from under the bonnet. I was going to bring those records down to my apartment when a better hiding place came to mind. I unlocked the nearby door to my garage and hid the files in the bottom of my toolbox, covering them with some newly laundered hand rags and a few odd parts from the TR. Then I took a very slow walk down to my apartment, pausing for a moment by B.J.'s door to listen. There was no sound. I would have felt better if I had heard her cry, letting out some of the hurt instead of leaving it to fester. But all was silent.

It was cold and foggy, a low, London-like fog, and the mournful blasts from foghorns in the bay suited my miserable mood perfectly. I lay abed listening for some sound from B.J.'s apartment above me but there was nothing. Maybe she was doing it on purpose, I thought, knowing that I'd be listening and determined not to give me the satisfaction of hearing her cry, the comfort of hearing some sign of life. I put it out of my mind to get some sleep. After all, I had to get up early for church in the morning.

I was up by seven but it took time to get a taxi. Apparently there had been a fire somewhere up near Coit Tower and the major streets below it were a tangle of emergency vehicles. When the taxi finally did get off the hill I had the cabby drop me at a rent-a-car place downtown. I picked up a sedan and drove down the peninsula to the First Church of Christ Militant, arriving just as the second service was letting out. I was startled to see the Rev. Robert Campbell greeting his parishioners as they filed out the door. I remembered his craggy, heavily lined face from our brief encounter in Alaska. Now, however, his shaved head was covered with a wig of wavy, black hair done up in the current blow-dried fashion. I lingered in the parking lot until most of his flock had gone, then ventured up to him. He recognized me immediately.

"I've been expecting you, Brother Peter. I hope you liked the service."

"Sorry, but I got here a little late, but then I don't go in much for religion."

"I don't hold with a lot of dogma myself. I preach the Gospel and I preach patriotism. I'm in the business of saving souls for the greater good of this nation."

"Saving it from communism, you mean."

"That goes without saying, Brother. Come around back where we can talk."

His office was in the parish hall. It was small and lined with bookshelves. His desk was a mess, covered with papers and periodicals and opened volumes. He motioned me to a chair and slid into his own behind his desk, pressing a button as he sat down.

"We're holding a training session this afternoon, Brother McCauley, so I'm glad you showed up. We'll get right to work and it's none too soon." A knock at the door interrupted him. "Come in, Brother Harold. Look who's come to worship with us. Brother Peter, I believe you've already met Deacon Harold Felkerson."

"Yes, we go way back, or so I'm told. We also were shipmates once, and more recently we met in a warehouse basement where he locked me in a storeroom while he inquired whether or not he should blow me away. The Lord be with you, Deacon."

Felkerson's eyes narrowed and if looks could kill my career as an Omega Force volunteer would have been over, right then and there. Without responding to me, he laid a canvas money bag on the desk, saying, "More than two thousand; a very good day."

"The Lord is smiling down on us, Deacon Harold. Lock it up and let us be about our worldly business. We've only got a few days to see how Brother Peter here will fit into our plans. First of all," he said, flipping his black robe up and over his head and slipping out of it, "we'll shift gears. This is a military mission and we're prepared to accept you at your current rank, Major McCauley. If you'll join us, we'll go next door to our little armory and get you properly outfitted. We're due in camp at three o'clock."

Next door to the church was the rectory, a Spanish-style home like many others in the neighborhood, dating from the early 1920s with adobe-colored walls and red tile roof. Behind it was a carriage house with servants' quarters on the top floor and a spacious garage below that had been converted into an arsenal and supply depot. While my hosts changed into their fatigue uniforms they turned me loose in the supply area and told me to select a uniform and boots appropriate for a field training exercise. When I was properly outfitted, Campbell brought out a cigar box filled with brass and dug up the gold leaf of a major and gave it to me along with an Omega symbol to complete my military attire.

"Each member of the force is responsible for his own uniform," Campbell said. "Now then, if you're ready we'll go into the rectory for lunch and then get underway."

We seated ourselves at a large dining room table and in a moment she came in carrying a tray with sandwiches, a pitcher of iced tea and a bowl of grapes. I must have looked startled at the sight of her.

"I see that you remember my wife, Major McCauley," Campbell said.

"Uh, why yes, I do. How are you, Mrs. Campbell?"

Mary smiled shyly and nodded to me as if nothing had ever transpired between us, while all I could think about was the wonderful time we had spent together in that cozy little cabin in the Alaskan wilderness, squeezing a year's worth of loving into a couple of hours. She was dressed sedately in skirt and blouse, but that fantastic figure was impossible to conceal. It was immediately apparent that not just Campbell himself had been privy to that Alaskan charade. She had been in on it, too, left behind to keep an eye on me while he came back to San Francisco to secure his grip on Omega Force without interference from Frank Carter. It probably was Mary who convinced him that I was indeed suffering from amnesia, and for that I was grateful. But I couldn't help but wonder if she was thinking about those wonderful sessions in the sack and on the bearskin rug in front of the fire. If she was, she didn't let on. As she left the room I caught sight of her marvelous rolling gait, the sensuous movement of her hips and bouncing of her beautiful red hair as she walked. I could feel Campbell's eyes on me and I wondered just how much he knew – or suspected. As it turned out, he was thinking about Alaska, too.

"I hope you aren't upset by our little deception, Major," he said. "But in times of a national crisis, we all have our calling. Even my wife."

Chapter 17

Felkerson's motor home with the dark tinted windows was waiting in the church parking lot. His wife barely looked up from her game of solitaire as we boarded. She was seated at a table near the rear of the vehicle, the air around her blue with smoke, her ashtray overflowing. Felkerson took the wheel while Campbell got into the passenger seat. I was relegated to the couch behind them. I had the feeling Felkerson's wife was watching me out of the corner of her eye, probably with her Saturday night special in her lap. I got the idea at Peabody's warehouse that she was itching for a chance to use it and I wasn't about to give her the opportunity. Besides, there was a lot to see and remember as we wound our way into the coastal mountains on a two-lane, twisting state highway. In an hour we turned off on a county road that took us away from the heavily timbered groves of redwood and madrone and into the higher elevations where live oak trees stood in stately isolation on the otherwise dry and barren terrain. At last we turned off on a gravel road that led us to a plush ranch-style home where a dozen or so cars and pickup trucks lined the driveway. Felkerson pulled his RV to a halt at the door and Campbell took off with great strides along a path that led toward the top a nearby ridge. Felkerson conferred briefly with his wife and then we took off at a jog to catch up with Campbell.

"Well, what do you think of it, McCauley?" the general asked, gesturing to the broad meadow that lay just below the ridge. In that field men in fatigues were engaging in hand-to-hand combat while three instructors in tee shirts moved among them. By actual count they numbered thirty, including the instructors. I couldn't wait to hear Campbell explain how he expected this handful of raw recruits to plunge this country into war, but I was willing to wait.

"So this is Omega Force," I said lamely.

"This is the cream of Omega Force," Campbell said proudly, "and fine men they are. They've been here since daybreak Saturday and will be here until sunset tonight. They're true patriots, every man a volunteer ready to give his life for his country. Yet tomorrow they'll be back in their own neighborhoods, getting up in the morning, going to work, caring for their wives and children, coming home at night to the bosom of their families, washing their cars, mowing their lawns. No one would ever suspect that each is a member of a well-trained combat team about to embark on the greatest assignment of his life. It's a privilege to command such men and a pleasure to welcome you to their ranks."

"And just how do you visualize my role, general? I'm afraid you may find me a little rusty after all these years."

"Initially you'll function as a spark plug, a role model. I shall depend on you to help set the example, to show these men how to conduct themselves in combat. Remember that none of them, with the exception of the three of us, has ever fired a shot in anger. Their enthusiasm is unquestioned, but they have no experience. It is up to us, to you and Colonel Felkerson and myself, to show them how to comport themselves in the face of the enemy. I have seen your reactions and I am convinced that you will be a model of courage, a paragon of self-control under the stress of combat. That's what they need, McCauley, someone to look up to, someone with backbone, nerves of steel."

"I only hope I can keep up with them, general. They're so...so young."

"There will be physical demands put upon you, undoubtedly. But you appear to be in pretty good shape. I know that your reflexes are extraordinary, well suited for the specific role I have in mind for you. Colonel Felkerson tells me you were very good at your work, so I'll leave you in his capable hands while I go down to inspire my men."

143

Felkerson snapped to attention and gave Campbell a sharp salute as the self-appointed general strode down the embankment toward the meadow.

"We observe military courtesy in the field, Major," Felkerson said will ill-concealed disapproval.

"Sorry, Colonel, but apparently saluting isn't one of my reflexive actions. You'll have to be patient until I can get the hang of it."

He was a humorless little man, much too old himself to be playing war games. I guessed he was crowding seventy, but wiry and hard as a rock. He began to walk along the ridge and I followed along and came up beside him. He spoke without looking at me.

"I understand what you've been through over the years with Colonel Ross," he said. "Despite his assurances that under the proper circumstances you will perform admirably, I don't mind telling I think you're unsuited for Omega Force. I didn't like what I heard about Alaska. You were slow, and it almost cost you your life. Your instincts were right, but the years have taken their toll."

"That's not very reassuring, Colonel. But with all due respect, sir, what do you know about my instincts?"

He looked at me at last and a curious little smile broke through the granite-firm frown he usually wore. "That's right," he said. "You don't remember Phoenix, do you?"

Phoenix! The name hit me like a punch in the stomach. While Felkerson launched into a diatribe on patriotism and the communist menace at our border, all kinds of bells began to reverberate in my brain, awakening nerve endings that had been dulled by many years of drugs and hypnosis. Slowly the deadened gray matter came to life with memories as fresh as yesterday. These weren't hallucinations. They didn't come in a terrible flash or as a confused kaleidoscope of overlapping visions. I was recalling events as any normal human being might recall them. And I knew immediately who Felkerson was – not a military officer at all, but a CIA agent, a cocky little bastard who sported a beret and a camouflage jacket

144

with a corduroy collar that looked as if it had come from Abercrombie and Fitch. He favored faded jeans and white socks and toted a Browning automatic pistol that was as pristine as the day some luckless GI dug it out of the Cosmoline and cleaned it for him. He strutted around like a bantam rooster and had a habit of barking orders. He was roundly hated by every soldier in the outfit, particularly me.

I'd been working as an advisor to the 2nd ARVN Division in Quang Ngai province and the Viet Cong had been making life miserable for us. Felkerson had come on quietly, first under cover as an AID employee, but later as chief coordinator of Operation Phoenix, the CIA program designed to neutralize the VC. My commander, Gen. Harrison Parks, assigned me to Phoenix out of sheer desperation. He could handle the politicians and the press, he said, but the dilettantes of the CIA were too much for him. My job was to get them off his back.

"It's a stinking, rotten job, but somebody's got to do it," he said. "Keep Felkerson under control. The goddamned spook thinks he's running the war! On the other hand, I can't have the VC in my rear. So do what has to be done and let's get it over with before we lose the whole god-damned war on the streets of Berkeley."

I was given command of a rag-tag band of ARVN non-coms and South Vietnamese irregulars and had set up a training program in counter-insurgency under Felkerson's direction. I had several junior officers on my staff and we used to laugh at how seriously Felkerson took his job. He was pompous, egotistical, outlandish in dress and behavior. He presented Operation Phoenix to us as if it was his own invention, when we knew damned well it had been passed down to him from some desk in Washington as the latest brainstorm to win the unwinnable war. It turned out to be little more than a covert campaign of assassination aimed at neutralizing the VC. We trained our Vietnamese irregulars to infiltrate villages to determine which peasants were VC or their sympathizers and to bring the information back to

145

Felkerson, who would plan raids to wipe them out. Combat teams then would storm the villages, usually in the dead of night, grab off a couple of VC to send back for interrogation, and kill the rest. Since none of them wore a sign saying, "I am a VC," a lot of innocent people were murdered. But that was not considered a problem. On the contrary, headquarters wanted body counts, the higher the better. We submitted off-the-cuff counts after each raid; Felkerson would increase our count by at least half, often adding our own casualties into the total, and send his report on up the line. He never once accompanied us on raids, but we knew first hand that those body counts included women and children, the old and infirm, anyone and everyone who might get caught in the crossfire. It was unavoidable, we told ourselves. When you hit a village there were going to be mothers and babies and children and old men and women, but never mind that, Felkerson would say.

"Those who are not engaged in guerrilla activities against us are providing cover for those who are. So what if they get in the way? They also get in the way of 500-pound bombs dropped from 30,000 feet. What's the difference?"

The difference was that killing them was a pretty grisly business, close-up and personal – grisly enough to drive a hardened combat veteran over the edge. As Felkerson droned on about Omega Force, I began to wonder why they had gone to all the trouble to erase such memories from my mind. Why did the Army think it was necessary to give me a new identity? My guess was that Ross only scratched the surface when he said it was because I had been good at my work, but at an awkward moment in history, whatever that meant. Why make me the object of complex scientific experiments, why me out of the many plagued by such memories? And if it were bad back then, why would anyone want to revive such "instincts" now? The Omega Force plan might hold the key.

"I'm grateful for the lecture on patriotism, Colonel, but I'd really like to know more about the operation, particularly my role in it," I said to Felkerson.

"I think it's safe now to give you a briefing. We're to gather here on Friday with full combat gear. We'll be issued small arms and provisions and motor to a rendezvous point where a cargo plane will meet us later that night to fly us to the combat zone. There we'll link up with local forces. For several weeks, perhaps even months, we'll be involved in training the locals for their role in our mission."

"What kind of mission?"

"Search and destroy. We're to find the enemy and kill him."

"But we're not at war with anyone that I know of," I said with intended naivete. That sent Felkerson into another dissertation on duty, with the implication that both God and country wanted me to kill the "enemy," war or no war.

"General Campbell will put you into the political picture later," he concluded. "Right now it's important to understand that our continent is on the verge of being taken over by communists and it's our job to prevent it."

"Do you really believe that a handful of men can confront an army, communist or otherwise? The Reds may be a menace, sir, but I read the newspapers. The leftists on this continent are armed to the teeth, if not by the USSR, then by China. You won't be facing a bunch of peasants, you'll be fighting the full might of international communism."

"Exactly!" he exclaimed. "You see, *I* remember Operation Phoenix. I know what a small clandestine combat unit can achieve when properly utilized."

"If memory serves, we didn't win that war."

"Don't crowd me, Major. General Campbell will brief you in good time. Meanwhile I want you to get acquainted with the men, familiarize yourself with their state of readiness, their general proficiency and their morale. Be on the lookout for two or three men you might wish to accompany you on your phase of the operation. That's all, Major."

I gave him a smart salute that he returned rather casually with a smug smile. Then I did as I was told, trying to keep out of the way of the trainees. They ranged in age from their middle twenties to the early thirties. Of the dozen or more I spoke to, none had had prior military experience, yet they seemed eager and confident. In another era they might have been revolutionary militiamen girded for battle against a repressive monarchy. But there was something disturbing about them, a lack of polish and cohesiveness. Despite their enthusiasm, they were still just a group of civilians playing war games, the type of men one might expect to answer a classified ad: "Adventure unlimited, no experience necessary." They got a thrill out of watching a cadreman show them how to slit a man's throat, but not one of them had ever done it and I doubted that in the heat of battle they could. Maybe that's what Campbell and Felkerson saw as my role, to set an example for these raw recruits, to instill in them the guts to do what has to be done to survive – and win. I'd have to be the first to fire my weapon, the first to draw my bayonet, the first to use it. The very thought gave me a feeling of uncertainty. I knew what combat was like, the pervasive fear of imminent death, my own or the other guy's. But I wondered if I could do it again. What if Ross had done his work too well? What if I didn't have it in me anymore? What if those "instincts" were gone forever? What if I couldn't pull the trigger? What if I froze at a critical moment? I'd be no better than these amateurs. It was a dangerous game they were playing and I wanted no part in it. I wanted out – as soon as I got a few more answers.

18 Chapter

Felkerson, the frustrated soldier and super-patriot spoiling for a fight, could be a very dangerous man, especially since he still had the ear of some powerful people at the agency. But however much he might wrap himself in the flag and cry out for communist blood, he still seemed to be a rational man, one who might listen to reasonable arguments against Campbell's mad scheme. The general himself was quite another case. He shared all Felkerson's dangerous tendencies plus one: His talked to God, or he thought he did.

"We've been looking forward to this day for a long time, Major McCauley," Campbell said after dinner. It was a cool, clear evening and we'd eaten barbecued chicken and macaroni salad around a fire pit on the Felkersons' flagstone patio. The self-styled commander had left his black hairpiece behind at the rectory and the flames playing on his heavily lined face and his bald head gave him a particularly sinister appearance. "Ross, for all his dedication, was the one weak link in our chain of command. He was a scientist, an intellectual, not a field soldier. But now you've come to us. You are the miracle God promised me. I knew the moment you appeared on the church steps this morning that my prayers had been answered."

"The colonel tells me you may let me in on my role in your operation, General. I hope that's the case, since I don't have much time to prepare."

"And so I shall, Major," he said, launching immediately into his dissertation. "Omega Force will gather here at five o'clock next Friday evening. Colonel Felkerson has arranged for two trucks and a jeep to meet us here. We will drive to the San Joaquin Valley by way of lesser-traveled roads to a ranch owned by good friends of mine who share our political philosophy. My friends were productive farmers once, but were bankrupted by the socialistic agricultural policies of the federal government and its confiscatory tax rates. There we will issue small arms and ammunition to the men while we await the arrival of a truckload of weaponry – shoulder-held surface to air missiles – to be delivered to us by some of our friends in The Group. At midnight a small transport plane will land at an airstrip especially prepared for us by my rancher friends. We will load our gear onto the transport plane that then will fly Omega Force to a secret airfield in a Central American nation currently ruled by a communist dictatorship. I feel it best not reveal the name of the country at this time in order to guard our fellow freedom fighters against any unfortunate turn of events. There's many a slip 'twixt cup and lip, as they say."

"I can understand your caution, General. I recall reading not long ago about some Stinger missiles that turned up missing during an inventory at a military base."

"Missiles and launchers, Major," Campbell elaborated. "And at that base now is a very wealthy supply sergeant who is due to retire soon and who then will vanish into a life of leisure. Meanwhile I fully expect those sophisticated weapons will be a major factor in turning the tide of war for our guerrilla friends south of the border. They in turn are expected to repay our kindness by loading our plane with cocaine in an amount yet to be negotiated."

"So your freedom fighters are buying Stingers with cocaine. I shouldn't think that would sit well with Washington. Or do I read the wrong news reports?"

"As I explained to you earlier," Felkerson interjected, "there are still some in Washington who share our views on the communist menace. Their support is surreptitious, but it is there and it is strong."

"It's simply capitalism at work," Campbell explained. "We buy weapons from The Group with cash, the freedom fighters by those weapons from us with cocaine, which we convert into cash to buy more weapons. And so it goes for as long as necessary."

"And how long do you figure that will be?"

"Until the United States government realizes that the only way to eliminate the cancer of communism is to meet it head on, until we engage it in battle and destroy it totally." Campbell slammed his fist into his palm for emphasis and his eyes took on an unholy glow. It didn't take a political genius to figure out what an impact supersonic missiles would have on international relations. As soon as those Stingers began blowing planes out of the sky – military or civilian – this country would be up to its ears in war.

"So you aim to let the hawks out of their cage, is that it?" I asked.

"And you're going to help, McCauley. We don't think that the introduction of strategically superior weapons alone will be sufficient to provoke the communists into a rash act of war. That's where you and your combat team come into play. Once our transport plane is safely en route back to the ranch in the San Joaquin Valley, we will begin training our guerrilla allies for a provocative attack on our enemies. You and your team will train for a related search and destroy mission. When you are proficient you will proceed to a small village in the mountains where our intelligence sources advise us a fiesta will be in progress. The country's president himself will be there to dedicate a new dam and power plant that promise to change the lives of the villagers forever. While Omega Force destroys the dam, you and your combat team will assassinate the president and his entourage."

I wanted to tell Campbell he was crazy, but I thought better of it. I wanted to live long enough to expose his scheme and hope that someone would care enough to stop it. I pressed him a little further to demonstrate my interest.

"And what about my combat team, General? How do we get out of the village after the raid? Or aren't we supposed to get out?"

"Why of course you are. We'll be in radio communication and you can rejoin us as soon as your task is completed. But does it really make any difference, Major? You have a rare opportunity to serve your country and perhaps find a place in its history books. What are you now, after all? You're nobody. You don't even exist. You have no official identity. It is as if you'd been erased from the face of the earth. If you're captured or killed, it won't make any difference. The very fact that you're recognizable as an American will be sufficient to elicit a belligerent response from the communists. They'll retaliate and war will be inevitable. Oh, McCauley, I've prayed over this many, many times and God has sent you to me. This is His will! Communism will be crushed forever in this hemisphere, perhaps even throughout the world. You and the brave Christian soldiers of Omega Force will be hailed as heroes for restoring the United States to a position of strength and moral leadership that is sorely needed in today's world. Praise the Lord, McCauley! Praise the Lord!"

Felkerson was looking a bit nervous, as if he were afraid Campbell's fervor might unsettle me. He spread out a map and began a detailed briefing.

"I think your chances of survival are extraordinarily good, Major. You've been through all this before. You have the skill; you will have the resources." Pointing at the map, he continued. "You and your team will be taken to this drop-off point by helicopter. You will make your way overland past this dam to the outskirts of this village during daylight hours. You'll reconnoiter the area, plan your attack and select your escape route before nightfall. After you have accomplished your mission you will withdraw immediately, return to the area of the dam, take cover and signal us by radio that you are in position. We then will issue orders regarding your role in our attack on that facility, which probably will come at daybreak."

152

"A textbook operation," I commented. "I understand I'm to train my own team, but will I have time to take them out on a dry run?"

"There should be plenty of time for that," Felkerson said.

"If everything goes smoothly," I pointed out. "I'm worried about those SAM missiles. If they're the ones stolen from that Army base, the feds are undoubtedly trying to track them. The boys at the Pentagon are touchy about who plays with their toys."

"You worry unnecessarily, Major," said the general. "We know our business."

"But can you trust your friends?" I asked. "If The Group lifted those Stingers, surely the feds are suspicious, particularly since they know The Group has taken over Omega Force. They may be on to you already. Who's supplying the transport from here to the valley? How do you know rendezvous ranch is safe? Your farmer friends could be under surveillance. And where's the plane coming from? It seems to me that a lot of people are involved in this shindig, and that means a lot of chances for slip-ups before we even cross the border."

"Good thinking, Major, but you must trust us," Campbell assured me. "We know who our friends are, and all possible precautions have been taken. I can't tell you more. I'm sure you understand the need for secrecy."

"The important thing," Felkerson added, "is whether we can count on your full cooperation. I surely hope so, because we have gone out on a limb by bringing you into the fold. I still have some last minute questions for Colonel Ross regarding his assessment of your integrity – I mean after all your so-called treatments. Nothing personal, of course, but some assurances from you also would be helpful."

"That's easy. I'll do my best not to disappoint you," I said. "And I'm sure the doctor will answer any questions you may have about me."

I had some questions for Ross, too, and I had no intention of taking off with these crazies on Friday night unless I got the answers. Meanwhile I was itching to tell someone about this madness before it got out of hand. And time was running short.

* * *

It was after midnight before I got back to the city. I crept down the steps to my apartment, tip-toeing by B.J.'s door just in case she was lying awake listening for me. One thing I didn't need right now was an emotional confrontation with a harebrained nymphomaniac. I unlocked my door and ran my fingers all around the frame to check for trip wires before easing it open quietly. Without turning on the lights I kicked back in my recliner and punched up Tobin's number. It rang eight times before he answered, sounding like a bear aroused from hibernation.

"It's me, Tobin, McCauley." There was dead silence on the other end of the line. "Are you all right, Tobin? Sorry if I awakened you, but I thought maybe you'd still be up."

"It really *is* you, isn't, McCauley?" he asked incredulously. "Forgive me, but I understood that you were dead."

"What do you mean, dead?"

"Your car, my friend, the Volkswagen."

"That's not my car; it belongs to a friend. What about it?"

"I regret to have to inform you, but I suspect then that your friend is dead. The car and everything in it was blown to kingdom come very early yesterday morning."

"My God, you can't mean that!"

"I'm afraid it's true. There was nothing left of the car but some odd bits of metal. What the explosion didn't destroy, the fire did. Very little remained but a scorched spot on the pavement."

"Where, how?"

"In that circular parking lot below Coit Tower. It apparently was a car bomb. I heard the radio traffic on my

154

police scanner and realized it was in your neighborhood. I got there an hour or so after it happened. All the police would say was that it appeared to have been a light blue Volkswagen and that one person died in it. The body parts were burned beyond recognition. There wasn't enough left to determine the sex let alone identity of the occupant. Forensics has the remains. After hearing the description of the car I cruised your area and couldn't find what I thought was your vehicle. And when you didn't answer your telephone all day, I came to the conclusion that you probably were the victim. I assumed that your mysterious assassins finally had caught up with you."

"Jesus, Tobin, what kind of maniacs are we dealing with? That was a poor, sick girl they killed. Do you understand? She was just a kid!"

"If it's any consolation, McCauley, she never knew what hit her. Look, it's been a very long day. Let me get some sleep and I'll get back to you, say around noon?"

"Yeah, okay, around noon."

I went immediately upstairs and let myself in to B.J.'s apartment. It was pretty much as it always was – dirty dishes in the sink, clothes scattered all over the place, the bed unmade. If she had been my daughter...

For some reason I found myself crying, blubbering like a broken-hearted kid, wondering why, oh, why did it have to be B.J.? Sure, she was troubled, really troubled, and she had done some pretty crazy things in her life, things most people would never understand, maybe even condemn. But it wasn't her fault. She wasn't responsible for how she turned out. At heart she was a good, generous kid who never hurt anybody. And she sure all hell didn't deserve to get blown to bits.

When the crying jag was over, I thought about the aftermath. They'd have an ID on her by now and tomorrow the cops would be swarming all over her apartment, digging into every facet of her life, checking out everyone she knew, including me. I used my tear-soaked handkerchief to rub my prints off the doorknob, then realized it didn't make much difference. My prints were all over her place and it wouldn't take a good cop long to match them with her downstairs neighbor. It might not tell them much, but it would link me to the case and there was no time to deal with them now. I'd have to get through to Kohler and ask him to keep them off my back – and tell him why. I returned to my apartment and stretched out on the bed, lying awake for a long time with a million thoughts running through my head. I was beginning to put the pieces of my past together, convinced now that someday it would all be there. I wanted desperately to know the truth, however awful it might be. I could tell it was going to be a bad night. I had an urge to put on the Beethoven tape, but I resisted the temptation. I didn't want to be lulled into complacency and forgetfulness, never again. I owed it to myself to be myself, no matter how much it hurt. And I owed it to B.J. to find out who planted the bomb that surely was meant for me.

I couldn't get to sleep, no matter what. A guy needed someone to talk to at a time like this, someone he could confide in, someone with a sympathetic ear, a soft shoulder to lean on. Naturally Cynthia Albright came to mind. She represented sanity, level-headed sanity. She had both feet on the ground, eyes wide open and no illusions. Once I had resolved to call her first thing in the morning, sleep came easy.

Chapter 19

The cops were at B.J.'s apartment promptly at nine o'clock and made no effort to keep their presence a secret. Their stomping around awakened me and I got angry at the thought of them pawing through her things, invading her personal life when she couldn't be there to protect herself. Later when this was all over maybe I could shed a little light on their murder case for them, but for now there wasn't a helluva lot I could do about it. I got up and shaved, showered and dressed in order to get out of there as quickly as possible. First, however, I had to call the cruise ship company in Seattle to see if they could tell me how to reach Cindy Albright. As I drifted ever closer to the eye of the storm I was becoming more and more obsessed with the idea of finding a safe haven, and Cindy stood out like a beacon of hope. The company gave me a mobile marine number and sure enough Cindy answered.

"This is Pete McCauley," I said, hoping she hadn't forgotten. "What's with this mobile marine number, do you live on a boat?"

"No, an island," she said. "Don't tell me, Pete – you've fallen out of another airplane."

"Not yet, but there's still a chance before the week is out. I've been meaning to get in touch, but I've been pretty busy since I got back to San Francisco. I didn't want you to think I'd forgotten you. I hope to get up your way before the snow flies. Maybe we can have dinner in the Space Needle."

"We don't have much snow up this way, and I'd avoid the Space Needle if I were you. That would be a pretty long fall, even for you." She punctuated that with a throaty laugh that made me want to crawl right through the telephone line to reach her.

"I'll take you anywhere you want to go," I said.

157

"Great! I've got some vacation time coming. I'll meet you at the ferry landing whenever you say."

"I'll call ahead. There are a lot of islands up there. What do you call yours?"

"Whidbey, but it really isn't all mine."

"Too bad, but I'm sure we can avoid those other folks. It'll be good to get away for a while."

"What's the matter, things not going well?"

"I suppose it could be worse," I said. "But I can't imagine how."

"Let me guess: An earthquake destroyed San Francisco and killed Clark Gable. Then Spencer Tracy turned his collar around and ran off with Jeanette MacDonald."

"Almost that bad. I'll bore you with the details later. I'll be away for a while, but I'll try to give you a call by the first of the month. If you don't hear from me…"

"What's the matter, Pete? I get the feeling you're in some kind of trouble. Is there anything I can do to help?"

"No, just be there for me, Cindy. Just be there."

* * *

I felt five hundred percent better after talking to her. All I wanted to do now was get this mess wrapped up and dumped in the garbage as soon as possible. I had to get in to see Ross again at San Francisco General before he became just another sad statistic in the AIDS epidemic, but first I had to bring Kohler up to date. He flipped on a tape to record my story and when he heard where his cocaine investigation had led, he flipped again.

"I can't believe it, McCauley."

"Believe it," I said. "You wanted to get Mr. Big? He's a wanna-be dictator hiding in some Central American jungle waiting for a chance to topple the lefties who run his country. Meanwhile he's knee-deep in the cocaine trade using rogue CIA operatives as his pipeline to the U.S. where whacko right-wing fanatics serve as the middlemen to the dealers for a cut of the profits."

"CIA operatives – it's incredible!" he said.

158

"Don't be naïve," I said. "You must read the papers – Allende in Chile, the Contras in Nicaragua, the kettle that's boiling now in Panama. There's a pattern there that even the Congress can't ignore any longer, and the fact that Latin America's top export crop is the prize shouldn't surprise anyone. Weapons cost money and there's always been a limit to how much the CIA can wring out of the politicians without stirring up the taxpayers."

"But you can't tell me that Ross can support all that skullduggery by peddling snow around the Castro."

"Of course, not. Ross is a nobody who probably skims a share of the dream powder to support his own habit, pay his medical bills and send his daughter to college. The heavy lifting is done by a nationwide network run by this outfit called The Group. They've got cells in every state, and when they're not running around in the boondocks playing war games, some of them support their fun with an occasional bank heist or by knocking over a liquor store. It's The Group that does the buying and selling. It used some of its cash to bribe an Army supply sergeant to get Stinger missiles and launchers for the whackos involved in this Omega Force operation. No, Ross might make a good witness, but he's far from being the top dog. But he is definitely a CIA operative who's been on the agency's payroll for years. He didn't run around dark alleys swapping matchbook covers with beautiful foreign agents. He's a medical doctor, a psychiatrist who specialized in curing crazies and developed a sideline by scrambling men's brains to see what kind of an omelet he could make. He thought of himself as a patriot serving his country under cover, but when he saw The Group taking over Omega Force he changed his mind. If he doesn't last long enough to testify for you, try a retired CIA agent named Harold Felkerson who's second in command of Omega Force. But the really dangerous character is Robert Campbell, long-time member of The Group and self-appointed commander of Omega Force. He's also a fundamentalist minister who talks to God and is certifiably insane."

"And this is the guy you say wants to get the U.S. involved in war?"

"That's his aim, but it's only an interim step. I think he ultimately wants to overthrow the government and set himself up as dictator. He's the hater-in-chief who dreams of a lily white nation of God-fearing fascists like himself."

"That would be impossible," Kohler shrugged in disbelief.

"Look, if he has Stinger missiles now, how long will it be before he gets his hands on an atomic warhead? He's got to be stopped, Kohler, and Friday's the deadline. Do you think you can do it?"

"I wouldn't know where to begin. I'm a narc, for Christ's sake. But I can send this tape through channels and see what happens. Maybe my boss can work something out with the U.S. Attorney. I'm sure the FBI and the ATF will want to become involved, not to mention the Pentagon. So you'll have to make yourself available, McCauley. They're going to have questions for you."

"I'm free until Friday, so work on it, Kohler, work on it as if my life depended on it, because I think it does."

* * *

I telephoned Dan Tobin just before noon and asked him to back me up later when I went to look in on Peabody. I didn't want the little creep to die strapped down in his own playroom – he'd qualify as a prime witness if this circus ever got closed down.

"Meanwhile," I said, "I'm heading for San Francisco General for a showdown with Ross. That latter-day Doctor Frankenstein has no excuse now not to play ball with me; I'm up to my ears in his little scheme with no apparent way to get out of it with my skin intact. It's time he gave me the answers I wanted."

I was surprised to find that Ross already had visitors. One was his wife and other I took to be his daughter. She

160

was around nineteen, with a pony tail and dressed in UC radical chic – beach walks and rolled up jeans, an oversized tie-dyed shirt and no bra, which in her case was a serious mistake. I was certain they thought I was one of Ross' boyfriends, but despite the hostility they exuded, I was impressed by their display of loyalty. I offered to come back later, but Ross wouldn't hear of it.

"He just wants some personal information and it won't take long," he told his family. "Wait out in the hall for a few minutes."

"Yeah, I'm just one of his patients," I explained.

"Well, he's not here to hold office hours," said the angry young girl. "Can't you see he's sick?"

"Come along, Laura, let's wait outside," said Mrs. Ross. "I hope you won't be too long, Mr. Harrison. It is Harrison, isn't it? David is very weak and we'd like a few more minutes with him."

"I won't be long," I assured her as she quietly closed the door.

"Interesting that you gave the name Harrison," Ross said.

"It just came to me."

"I suppose you've told Felkerson about me."

"No, I've told him as little as possible. But I know he's been trying to get in touch with you. He said he still had a few questions about me before we embark on World War III. I'll be going along as a hired gun, but not before I get some answers of my own."

"Thank God you're going, McCauley. I'm counting on you to keep this operation focused on the training of indigenous troops. It can't be allowed to reach a combat phase. We've got to keep Omega Force clean, just as Gen. Harrison Parks would want it. It's interesting that you used his name in concealing your identity. He'd be pleased. You were the son he never had. He was devastated when you went to pieces in Vietnam. He blamed himself, of course, but there was little he could do under the circumstances. Reports

161

on the My Lai massacre were on the news broadcasts every night. Rumors of an Army cover-up were rampant and an investigation was inevitable. He knew that in comparison to what you had done in Operation Phoenix, My Lai would look like a Sunday school picnic. And there you were, out of your head, raving your guilt to the world. He had to keep you quiet and the CIA was only too happy to oblige."

"Felkerson, right?"

"Harold knew of my work and told Parks about it. The general had you placed under my care while I was still in Vietnam. You were a mess, McCauley, a real challenge. I treated you as best I could under the circumstances – sedation, mainly, until I could bring you back to Letterman. Once we got here I tried several different methods in an effort to wash away your memories and your guilt, but nothing worked for long. Then something happened that gave me an idea for a new approach – transplanting personalities. Another officer under my care died suddenly in a drowning accident. In closing out his file I noticed the similarity in your backgrounds: You both were orphans with no connections outside the Army. I wondered if, after erasing your past, I could implant the details of his life in your mind. It might prevent the recurrence of your problem. I'd make you Peter J. McCauley."

"Instead of...?"

A troubled look came over his ravaged face, as if he were still reluctant to tell me the whole story. Then he shrugged, indicating that it made no difference to him now.

"Your real name was Paul Joseph Mahon," he said at last.

That was it! That was the last piece of the puzzle. It all made sense to me now, but I'd be damned if I'd give Ross the satisfaction of my true reaction. He might have more information in that sick mind of his, so I deadpanned his stunning revelation and let him go on, the gorge rising in my throat.

162

"As a young officer in Korea you were awarded the Distinguished Service Cross. During the dark days of that war you were sent home to a hero's welcome and all its attendant publicity. Later in Vietnam you again distinguished yourself, winning a Bronze Star for valor. Your story was sent out over the news wires in an effort to counter-balance the antiwar demonstrations at home. So when you broke down, General Parks wanted your condition to remain a secret. He listed you as missing in action and turned you over to me."

Mahon and Parks – I should have put it together earlier, but Ross had done his work well. Earlier, those names in conjunction meant nothing to me; now they filled me with rage. I wanted to throttle him, to wrap my fingers around his scrawny throat and squeeze the life out of him. I could see he was studying my expression, looking for some glimmer of response. In his twisted mind, this was the final test of his greatest experiment. He wanted to see if I had any recollection of my past life, if I would recognize my own name. Here he was, dying of an incurable disease and more interested in his monstrous accomplishment than in the Grim Reaper. I decided to let him gloat. He might tell me more that I should know.

"The name doesn't mean anything to you, does it," he said exultantly. "You don't remember Paul Mahon, do you?"

"I don't know if you're telling me the truth or lying to get me off your back, Ross. If it's true, why was it so important to eliminate Paul Mahon?"

"Because he had become a tragic embarrassment. He had been a hero when the nation didn't have many heroes. And now he was a raving maniac, railing against the terrible atrocities of the war. If his story had gotten to the public there would have been an even greater outcry against our involvement in Vietnam. Parks took his dilemma all the way to the Pentagon. The order came back that Paul Mahon was to be silenced in the most humane manner possible."

163

"You mean kill him?" I was shocked, and it didn't help that we were discussing Mahon in the third person. It reinforced my sense that I was little more than a helpless guinea pig in Ross' macabre laboratory.

"There are other ways of silencing a man, McCauley. Parks never would have been so callous. He wanted very much to keep Paul Mahon alive in hopes of a cure. That's why he listed him as an MIA and turned him over to me."

"Why so sentimental? Parks was a combat officer, used to death in all its grisly forms. Why didn't he get rid of Mahon permanently? You could have given him a dose of something from your medicine bag and solved all Parks' problems."

"There were two good reasons to keep him alive. From my standpoint, Mahon presented a challenge, an excellent subject for my experiments. But more importantly, Parks felt personally responsible for his breakdown and wanted desperately to see him cured. You see, McCauley, Paul Mahon was more than a surrogate son to the general – he was his son-in-law. Not only had he married Parks' daughter, but together they had given the general a grandson. The poor old man spent the remainder of his life hoping I could cure Mahon and return him to the bosom of his family. But it was not to be. In curing him, I in effect destroyed him and left you in his place. Once he had become mentally stable as Pete McCauley, he had no recollection of his wife and son, let alone General Parks."

I knew at last why the name Mahon had stirred me so when I read about Parks' daughter and her son in the general's obituary, and that empty feeling in my gut when I read later that they had died in the bombing at the Parks estate. I was reading about the murder of my own family. My anger was becoming impossible to restrain.

"You filthy pervert, Ross! Who gave you the right to play God? How can you stand to live with yourself?"

He smiled wanly at the unintentional irony of my remark.

"If I have sinned, McCauley, I am paying for it now a thousand times over. But don't blame me for the death of your family. I think you settled that score when you shot Frank Carter to death in Alaska."

"But I didn't know," I said. "You even denied me the satisfaction of vengeance."

"There's nothing more to tell now, McCauley. Go away and leave me in peace. Send in my wife and daughter. I've made amends; I've been forgiven. We're determined to face this crisis together. When you're at death's door, it's comforting to know that someone still cares about you, despite the wrongs you've done them."

"I'll bet that it is, Ross. It's a feeling I'll never know, thanks to you."

Chapter 20

I was surprised to find Tobin waiting for me outside the hospital, double-parked and creating a one-man traffic jam. He was squeezed behind the wheel of his Oldsmobile like a motorized Buddha, leaning on his horn to attract my attention. I barely heard him above the noise of all the angry drivers honking at him.

"Get in, McCauley. It occurred to me that you might need a lift, since your friend's car was demolished. Is Peabody next on your agenda?"

"I want to look in on him. I left him trussed up in his playroom all weekend and he's probably getting pretty ornery by now. After that, I'd like to spend some time going over Ross' file on Peter J. McCauley. Could be I can turn up some information that would help you in that inheritance case. If you could prove that McCauley is dead, the executors might be able to have the body exhumed for a positive identification. I don't know the law, but it seems to me that McCauley's natural son ought to get a piece of that $300,000."

"Yes, of course. But I thought you said the McCauley file was in the car that was bombed."

"I took it out and stashed it in my garage the night before the blast."

"I see. Well, that file might indeed be of some value to Ms. Carey and her son. I wonder if you'd allow me to see it."

"First things first, Tobin. I think we ought to look in on Peabody, don't you?"

"Yes, yes, of course. I suppose we should."

He chugged down Potrero Avenue and headed toward Civic Center, the Olds spewing a cloud of black smoke until the moment it lurched up to a parking space on Van Ness Avenue. The Opera Plaza with its array of shops, restaurants, office suites and theater, was a popular place on a Monday afternoon. As we crossed the plaza I looked up and saw Peabody looking down on us from the mezzanine. He was disheveled and wild-eyed as he leaned over the railing, seeming to point at us. Then a shot rang out and I heard the twang of a bullet smacking the concrete in front of us.

"Get down!" I shouted, shoving Tobin's great bulk behind a circular fountain and diving there for cover myself. Everyone in the plaza seemed to freeze at the sound of the shot, but apparently no one else had seen Peabody fire. "Take cover!" I yelled. "There's a man on the mezzanine firing a weapon!"

Once they got the message all hell broke loose. People were screaming and darting for cover. From the shops the curious wandered out to see what the fuss was all about and I heard someone shout, "Call 911! There's a man up there with a gun!"

Peabody fired again and this time the bullet slammed into the fountain just above our heads, showering us with fragments of stone and concrete. Tobin winced, fished around inside his coat, pulled out a .38 and handed it to me.

"Take it, take it! I'm scared to death of guns."

He rolled away from me and pressed his fat body as tightly as he could against the base of the fountain while I slowly raised my head. Peabody was still on the mezzanine, his revolver poised for another shot. When he spotted me he aimed and fired again. I heard the bullet plunk into the fountain pool and at that instant I made a dash for the open stairway that led to the mezzanine. He fired again as I ran, but he missed and the bullet ricocheted off the concrete and smashed into a restaurant window. I heard screaming inside as the glass shattered but I didn't look back. I raced up the stairs two at a time and took cover on the landing out of Peabody's line of sight, but where I could look down on the plaza. In the distance I could hear sirens. The cops would be there momentarily, I figured, so I waited, reluctant to stick my neck out. As I watched the plaza Tobin looked up, apparently realized he was alone out there, and began to crawl away from the fountain. He was a ridiculous sight, bellying along like some great wallowing beast. I was about to yell at him to stay under cover when another shot rang out and he collapsed in a heap. That was enough for me. I dashed up the next flight of stairs to the mezzanine and came out on Peabody's level just as he ducked behind a divider wall that surrounded a swimming pool. High above him in the towers faces began to appear in windows as the apartment dwellers looked out to see what was going on. Two children who had been swimming in the pool walked deliberately across the area between us, the boy with his arm protectively around the shoulders of his little sister. Peabody, sitting on a lounge chair to reload his revolver, ignored them. Behind me a security guard, his back pressed to the hallway wall, edged cautiously toward me.

"Don't shoot," he whispered nervously. "Don't shoot. That's Mr. Peabody out there. He's not himself. He may hurt someone."

"Not if we can stop him," I said.

"Look out! He's coming this way!" the guard shouted.

Peabody suddenly appeared in front of the waist-high divider wall that surrounded the pool. He was only ten feet from me, clutching his revolver with both hands and aiming it at me. Responding as if to habit, I hit the deck and rolled into the prone position with Tobin's .38 pointed at Peabody's head. He got off the first round, the bullet slapping the concrete between my outstretched legs and whistling away. I fired at almost the same instant. Peabody dropped his weapon and grasped his throat with both hands. Blood oozed from between his fingers and he fell to his knees, staring at me with a dead man's eyes. Then he pitched forward with a weird gurgling sound and lay very still in a widening pool of blood. Two cops were on the scene in moments with their service revolvers drawn. One took Tobin's .38 carefully from my hand while the other checked Peabody for a pulse.

"Wasted," he said.

"Stand up slowly, fella. Hit the wall and spread 'em," said the other.

"The guy was berserk," I said. "I shot in self defense. Ask the security guard."

"We'll see about that," said the cop as he patted me down. "Now give me one hand at a time."

In a flash he had the cuffs on me and was leading me down the stairway to the plaza where a crowd had formed around Tobin.

"That's my pal who was hit," I told the cops. "Give me a second to talk to him."

Paramedics were rolling him over and I couldn't see any blood until he spoke. Then a small trickle of it ran from the corner of his mouth.

"He shot me, McCauley," he gasped.

"Why in hell didn't you stay put?" I asked angrily.

"I was frightened. I was alone out there. Why did he shoot me?"

"I don't know," I said quietly. "Maybe you were just too big a target to resist."

The cop jerked me away and dragged me toward the Van Ness exit where his black and white was waiting at the curb with its lights flashing. He helped me into the back seat as two back-up patrol cars and an ambulance screamed up. Shouting over the din, the cop read me my rights and I exercised the one about remaining silent. In the booking room I used my one telephone call to reach Kohler.

"Not again!" he exclaimed. "What's the charge this time?"

"They haven't told me yet, but it's okay. Somehow I figure I'll be safer in jail."

"You've got a thing about you, McCauley. You attract trouble like a magnet. Just keep cool. I'll be down within the hour. I've got people coming all the way from Washington to talk to you about your weekend outing. Wait'll I tell 'em you almost got your ass shot off before the war began."

* * *

There were about twenty people in the conference room. They represented the FBI and Treasury out of Washington, sheriff's deputies from San Mateo County, SFPD and a lone gray eminence who sat out the introductions, lingering in the background and never saying a word throughout the discussion, which went on well into the wee hours. I knew he must be CIA, and to test my theory I made it a point to watch his expression when I mentioned the super-spooks and their role in the cocaine trade. But he really winced only once – when I threw in Felkerson's name. That was enough to confirm my suspicions. I couldn't tell what he was up to, but the others in the room were formulating a plan to block the Omega Force operation, to close it down for good and along with it the gunrunners from The Group. The guy I took to be CIA took voluminous notes during the discussion and I hoped he was on our side when the chips were down. I had reason to wonder about him, since Ross had indicated there were elements within the agency that supported the Omega Force concept.

After outlining the operation as I understood it I took a few questions from around the table, then sat back as the lawmen began formulating a plan for intervention.

"With all due respect," said one young FBI agent, "I don't think Mr. McCauley should take part in this discussion for security reasons. What if his, uh, colleagues discover where he's been tonight? It might place him in jeopardy, or at the very least make life very uncomfortable for him. I suggest it's time he be excused."

There followed a general buzz of agreement, and I got up to leave as the agent asked: "Are there anymore questions for Mr. McCauley?"

"I have one," said an AFT agent. "Will Omega Force be carrying ammunition or explosives at the time it departs from the Felkerson property?"

"Side arms, M16s and hand-to-hand combat equipment – knives, choke wires," I said, "along with some ammunition. The heavy stuff is to be issued at Rendezvous

Ranch, including anti-tank weapons and Stinger surface to air missiles and their launchers."

"Then we've got to take them before they leave for the ranch," said a deputy. "It would be safer."

"But we've got to wait until the SAMs arrive," said an ATF agent. "We want those weapons and the men who appropriated them."

"How about simultaneous strikes," said the young FBI agent.

"Pretty difficult to coordinate," said the ATF man. "The timing is indefinite. We don't know when the trucks will reach the staging area."

"It's my opinion that we reserve discussion of tactical matters until after Major McCauley has been excused," the FBI agent said.

Kohler took me by the elbow and guided me toward the door.

"I'd give my right arm to know the final plan," I said when were out in the hall.

"And have Campbell and his men kick it out of you?" Kohler asked. "The FBI is right – what you don't know can't hurt you."

"In that case, if you don't need me any longer, I think I'll stop for a bite to eat and then check on Tobin. He's been a big help lately and I want to be sure he's okay."

"You'll probably find him at Mission Emergency. Tell you what, give me a call after you eat and meantime I'll get a condition report on him. No use wasting your time if you can't get in to see him."

I hopped a cab for North Beach and dropped by the Tosca for a couple of martinis. It was almost closing time and the place was nearly empty, but I didn't care. The martinis weren't for socializing, they were to dull my brain and sharpen my appetite. They did a good job of both. Later I ambled down Broadway to Vanessi's and ordered a Joes's Special for dinner. Someone had left an early edition of the Chronicle on the counter and I read it while I ate a big plate of eggs scrambled with ground beef, spinach and mushrooms all laced with fresh garlic. The paper said the cops had identified one Barbara Jean Franklin, 22, a telephone company employee, as the victim of the car bombing early Sunday morning. Amid the usual comments of the police and fire officials I came across some speculation that the job had been done with dynamite and a heat-sensitive fuse, probably wired to the VW's exhaust pipes. Those pipes would have gotten red hot during the drive up Telegraph Hill Boulevard. But no one knew who had done it or why. The police were still working on it, the article said.

Two columns of space were devoted to the story, plus a large photograph of the blast scene and a mug shot of B.J. that looked as if it might have been her high school graduation picture. The story said police had found a vial of Valium in her apartment, but that any evidence of drug use would have to await the autopsy report. I lost my appetite and pushed my plate aside. It irritated me that drugs were automatically presumed to play a role in any crime. I knew B.J. was no junkie. She was just a poor, mixed up kid who'd been dealt a bad hand in life and finally cashed out in a tragic case of mistaken identity. It was well after midnight by now, so I gave Kohler a call to see if I could get in to see Tobin.

"I wouldn't advise it," he said. "He's still alive, or he was an hour ago, but if he's your pal, you don't need any enemies. Why don't you come on down and we'll talk about it. There are some things you might be able to clear up for us."

Kohler said the cops had gotten to Tobin at the hospital and told him he was going to die. And with a bullet in his lung, Tobin believed them. He had a lot on his conscience and wanted to clear it before he met his maker, so he spit out a lot more than blood.

"He was just a third-rate private investigator, you know, McCauley. He had a reputation for picking up two-bit cases off the police blotter and running them down for whatever few bucks might be in it for him."

"So what? That isn't against the law."

"You're right. But murder is, and that's why Tobin's going to be booked," Kohler said, looking very cop-like and omniscient.

"Bullshit. He wouldn't hurt a fly," I protested. "He didn't even know how to use the .38 he carried."

"Maybe so, but he knew something about dynamite. He claims he's responsible for that car bombing Sunday and he says it was aimed at you. You can read his statement over at homicide, if you want. Maybe you can shed some light on their case. Tobin says Peabody paid him for the job, but we can't question a dead man."

I read Tobin's statement reluctantly. I'd grown to like the guy and it hurt to think he'd been willing to blow me to kingdom come for a few lousy bucks. But I should have guessed. He was a cheap hustler who leached a living from other people's miseries. To a low-life like him I was nobody, while Peabody was the pot of gold at the end of the rainbow. All he had to do was offer his services. He didn't have the guts to gun me down, but dynamite on a hot muffler could do the job. No wonder the fat man was so surprised when I telephoned him Sunday night. He'd probably been expecting the payoff call from Peabody, and instead he hears his "victim" on the other end of the line. I can imagine the rest: Tobin probably had followed me to Peabody's apartment, set him free after I left and offered his services. They hatch a deal and Peabody's furious when Tobin tells him later that I'm still alive. He orders him to bring me down to the Opera Plaza so he can do the job himself. Tobin shows up at San Francisco General, offers me a lift and tries to put his finger on the McCauley file in case Peabody cancels his payoff. After all, a guy's got to make a living and that inheritance case was still open. He never suspects that Peabody would try to kill him. Too bad he didn't. Tobin would be better off dead than spending the rest of his life behind bars.

Chapter 21

I wanted to sleep in Tuesday morning, but my luck was running true to form. The FBI called at eight. They wanted to talk about Conrad Peabody III and asked me to meet them outside the old swim club at Aquatic Park as soon as possible. I told them eleven would be about as soon as possible, since I was still half asleep.

They were waiting for me, looking like two door-to-door missionaries in their cheap suits, button-down collars and conservative ties. I wondered idly where they'd parked their bicycles. The older one was the same agent who had conducted the strategy meeting last night. In his deference to his boss the younger man gave the impression of being a trainee on his first outing. We walked into the center of the green that stretched from the bayside to Beach Street and Ghirardelli Square and sat down casually on the grass.

"We were reviewing an interesting case this morning, Mr. McCauley – a shooting at the Opera Plaza yesterday. We understand you may know something about it."

"Correct," I said. "But what makes it a federal case?"

"The victim was under federal investigation."

"Peabody?"

"The Group is one of our active files, so naturally we were curious. Especially since you already had described its role in your weekend plans. We think it's interesting that Mr. Peabody should come to a violent end at your hands just before you got involved in a critical situation with his organization."

"You mean you think I blew it?"

"Not necessarily. We believe their plans will go forward, but in all probability without you."

"If you think they're going to bump me off in retaliation, not to worry. They were planning to do that long before my run-in with Peabody. They're just waiting for the right moment. They won't hit me as long as they think I still can be of some value to them."

"Then you're fully aware of the dangers involved. We had come to warn you. Mr. Evans here is in charge of the West Coast investigation of The Group. He can explain."

"You killed their San Francisco leader, Mr. McCauley," said Evans, who didn't look old enough to be in charge of anything. "And now, as I understand it, you're closely involved with Peabody's boss. Campbell, you see, is in charge of the Western division, which includes sixteen states including Alaska and the Hawaii. He has managed to draw together all sorts of organizations that we think could pose a threat to the national security – paramilitary, terrorist, survivalist and political groups. United under his leadership they comprise The Group. They all have one thing in common: avid anti-communism. And anyone who is not with them one hundred percent is considered by them to be a communist. Many of the widely scattered units have their own version of Omega Force, which they use against targets that help finance their operations. We're talking armed robbery here – banks, armored cars, liquor stores, gun shops. In metropolitan areas they're dealing in drugs; some are reportedly engaging in terrorist activities as a form of political expression. As a matter of fact political assassinations may be next on their agenda.

"Campbell encourages them to adopt the omega symbol as sort of a secret password, as it were – omega, the end. They see themselves as the final solution to the world's problems, which is how Campbell views Omega Force. He has an edge on the rest because Omega Force was founded with a certain government legitimacy that the others lack. But he has perverted its original purpose and turned it to his own use. We agree with you that he must be stopped, and it appears to us that his plans this weekend may be our last and best chance to stop him. The Stinger missiles make it all the

175

more urgent. They must not be allowed to fall into the wrong hands. Of course, we need your help."

"You'll have it," I said. "It should be easier for you with me on the inside. But if they find out that I killed Peabody, I'm afraid it's all over."

"Your tracks already have been covered up, Mr. McCauley," said Evans. "But you'll have to be on your guard. The Group is a very dangerous outfit, worse than the mob – better lines of communication, more sophisticated weapons. If they have any inkling that you're not with them one hundred percent, they'll not hesitate to kill you."

"How do you know they haven't already connected me to the Peabody killing?"

"We *don't* know. We put a lid on the case immediately, but you can never be sure. We don't know, for instance, if one of the responding officers might be a member, or if some member might have witnessed the shooting. You'll have to take that chance."

"What about Tobin, the fat guy who took a slug during the shootout. Someone might get to him."

"No problem there, McCauley. Tobin died early this morning."

"Tobin's dead? That's too bad." It didn't matter that Tobin had gotten a little greedy and tried to blow me away. Fact is, with B.J. dead, the fat man was the only friend I had in the world and I'd taken a liking to him.

"Is there anyone else who might link you to Peabody?" Evans asked.

"There's Doctor Ross – I'm sure Kohler told you about him. And Campbell, of course, and his second in command, Felkerson, Harold Felkerson."

The agents exchanged grim smiles at the mention of Felkerson's name, but their only advice was, "Keep on your toes, McCauley."

It was clear to me that my safety wasn't their top priority, but I appreciated the warning nonetheless. They gave me a contact number and that was the end of it. I walked them up to the cable car turnaround where they boarded a Hyde Street car, sticking out like two sore thumbs amid a clutch of tourists. I took a hike down Beach Street and cut over to Fisherman's Wharf for a walking crab cocktail, thinking all the while about Dan Tobin and poetic justice and wishing B.J. hadn't gotten in the middle of all this. I tossed my oyster crackers one at a time out over the water and watched the seagulls snatch them in mid-air, then elbowed my way out of the thickening crowd of tourists. As I walked along The Embarcadero I glanced up at Coit Tower atop Telegraph Hill, and couldn't help thinking about the car bomb and what it must have done to that poor kid. By the time I reached Pier 23, my favorite watering hole, I was ready for a cold martini and some hot jazz piano. By the time the joint closed it was dark and I was blind, stinking drunk.

I remember climbing the wooden steps up the backside of the hill, stumbling now and then and having a helluva time getting up again. I remember fumbling with my latchkey, staggering through my darkened apartment and sprawling on my bed fully clothed. I slept the clock around, a deep untroubled sleep that lasted until my telephone rang that afternoon.

"Felkerson," barked the voice on the other end of the line. "Where in hell have you been?"

"None of your damned business," I moaned.

"I've been trying to get you, Major."

"I've been busy."

"For two days and nights?"

"I didn't know you were keeping track."

"I've got some business in the city tomorrow. The general wants you to have dinner with us tomorrow night. We have to load the equipment for Friday. I'll drop by and pick you up."

"What time?"

"Two o'clock at Union and Montgomery."

"I'll be there."

He hung up without another word. I wondered if he was coming to San Francisco to see Peabody or Ross and if he knew about them, knew that one was dead and the other one dying. I wondered if he knew I had the world's worse hangover or that I'd be lucky to be alive tomorrow at two. After some aspirin and a cold, cold shower I decided I didn't give a damn what Felkerson knew about Ross or Peabody or me, for that matter. I knew he hated my guts and wanted me dead, but he was stuck with me now. Crazy Campbell thought I was a Godsend, and that would keep me safe for the time being. Felkerson would never question a commander who had a direct line to God.

Once my eyeballs shrank back into their sockets I downed a mug of strong, black coffee and fortified myself with a big breakfast. I wanted a clear head when I went out to do some research. I had to find out all I could about Paul J. Mahon and whether I could ever be him again or if it was my fate to be Pete McCauley forever. I spent more than an hour in my garage, seated in the TR3 and going through the fat file that Ross had accumulated on us – or me. He was right about one thing: There were a lot of similarities in our backgrounds that made it easy for him to switch our lives around. But his notes only scratched the surface – lots of facts, but nothing deep or personal. In frustration I laid the file aside. I wanted to know more about my wife and son. Strange, I thought, how the prospect of short future sharpens a guy's curiosity about his past.

At the public library I found several listings in the Readers Guide to Periodical Literature for General Parks, mainly in news magazines ranging from the 1950s to the 1980s, the most recent the reports on the explosion that destroyed his estate and his family. Two of the listings made reference to Paul Mahon, so I checked them first. One was a June 1952 article in Liberty magazine, part of a story about heroes of the Korean War. A couple of paragraphs were devoted to Lt. Paul Joseph Mahon of Omaha and the exploits that won him a couple of medals and a field commission.

The face in the thumbnail photograph clearly was mine. I made a few notes and figured I'd go to Omaha someday to see if there were any Mahons around who might claim me. I found the second Mahon reference in a Life magazine pictorial layout featuring General Parks shortly before he shipped out for Vietnam. Featured among the events that preceded his departure was the wedding of his daughter, Elizabeth, to his aide de camp, Captain Paul J. Mahon. The photographs included several from the reception, including one of the general offering his sword to the happy couple to slice their wedding cake. *"General's Daughter Weds War Hero,"* said the headline. I couldn't take my eyes off her. She was indescribably beautiful. The shock of seeing the two of us together finally broke down the barriers Ross and his experiments had erected in my mind. I remembered everything about her now, from our first meeting in Paris between wars when she and her mother, a Japanese war bride, attended a NATO party for European diplomats in 1956. I didn't want to go, but the general insisted – he had security matters to attend to, he said, as he ordered me to pick up the ladies at their hotel and escort them to the party. Only later did I find out that the wily old codger had set the whole thing up to bring Elizabeth and me together. It worked. She was only a kid then, but I fell for her, fell hard. I could see now as I looked at that picture spread why I'd freaked out at the sight of that family at the Jacuzzi aboard the cruise ship – the Caucasian father, the beautiful Eurasian mother and their handsome young son. My screwed up brain was trying to tell me something that day, trying to make me remember my own past. The experience that day had made me dizzy; now it only made me sad, profoundly sad. I recalled our brief honeymoon in a rustic cabin on the shores of Cultus Lake in central Oregon's Cascade Mountains. I remembered canoeing to a intimate little cove on the opposite side of the lake, of swimming in the frigid waters and lying in the warm afternoon sun with the world far away. I remember returning there two years later when I was on rotation from Vietnam, reliving the whole beautiful experience. And I remembered her telling me just before I shipped out again that she was pregnant and was going to miss me terribly and to take care. "Please be careful, because I love you so," she said. I remembered it all now, the laughs we had, the love we shared. Oh, God, how I remembered.

I don't know how long I drifted through the memories of those happy days as I sat clutching that musty old magazine, but I awakened only when a young librarian came to my side and gently shook me.

"I'm sorry, sir, but are you all right?"

"What? Oh, I must have fallen asleep. I hope I didn't disturb anyone."

"Oh, no, not at all. We just wanted to be sure you were okay."

She went away then and I realized my neck was sore from dozing with my chin on my chest. My eyes seemed raw and I noticed that teardrops had marked the page of the magazine that lay open on the table. I got one of those stubby little pencils they use at libraries and a scrap of paper and wrote down the name and date of the magazine and brought it to the return desk. Maybe I'd come back someday and look at it again, I thought.

* * *

Felkerson was right on time. His big RV came lumbering up the Union Street hill like some demon vehicle out of a futuristic horror film, all dark and ominous and foreboding. I waited on the corner until he had made his turn-around before I got in.

"What's in the bag?" he demanded.

"Toilet kit, change of underwear, socks and the morning newspaper. You want to go through it?"

"No. What do you know about Ross? When did you see him last?"

"I don't know, a few days ago, I guess."

"We can't find him. He's cleared out of Letterman and he's not at home. No one seems to know where he is, or so they say. They know where he is, all right. I think they may be on to us."

"Who are *they*?"

"Never mind. Did you read about Peabody? He's dead. Apparently went berserk and turned his apartment building into a shooting gallery. He killed a man before the cops got him. You know anything about it?"

"Just what I read in the papers."

"Curious. Witnesses said someone was arrested, but the cops say they have no suspects. Very curious. I'm going to recommend we call off the operation."

"Why? What's Peabody got to do with the operation?"

"Nothing. He didn't know a thing about it. But whoever shot him might have been working under cover. That would mean they're getting close. If I could find Ross I'd feel a lot better. You're sure *you* haven't seen him?"

"Not since my last appointment. He seemed okay then."

"He didn't say anything that made you suspicious?"

"I'm not the suspicious type, Colonel. I take things as they come and I don't ask a lot of questions. I avoid a lot of trouble that way."

"Perhaps, but sometimes it's prudent to be suspicious. That's why I don't trust you, McCauley. I never had much faith in Ross' experiments, and as far as I'm concerned that's all you are – an experiment that should have been terminated a long time ago. Experiments have a way of going wrong at awkward moments."

I didn't like the way he used the word terminated, but I was getting used to living on the edge where Felkerson was concerned. I couldn't conceal my contempt for him.

"I follow orders and I do my job," I snapped. "That was the deal. I'll jump through your hoop on cue, but meanwhile lay off, find something else to worry about." The guy made my skin crawl and I was more certain than ever that it was Felkerson who'd been trying to knock me off ever since the Alaska fiasco. It would be easier for him with me out of the way. Then he could tell Campbell, "See, I told you so. McCauley was dirty and needed to be scrubbed. We'll be

181

better off without him." But as long as I was alive I was Campbell's sign from on high, and Felkerson couldn't argue with divine guidance.

It was late afternoon when we reached the church. Campbell was at his office door, chatting amiably with a group of parishioners. We sat in the RV in the parking lot until he was alone at last and signaled us to join him.

"Sorry to keep you waiting," he said. "I was just laying out plans for the operation of the church during my absence. An extended vacation, I told the vestry. Now let's get your RV into the garage and get it loaded."

We spent the next hour stowing away M16 automatic rifles, cases of .30 caliber ammunition and several crates of hand grenades. Campbell checked everything off his list and updated his inventory records. I knew Felkerson was itching to make one last pitch to leave me behind, so I stayed close by so I could butt in, if necessary. But Felkerson was strangely tight-lipped, not even mentioning Ross or Peabody. He was probably smart to keep his mouth shut. Campbell's enthusiasm was at a high pitch and there was no telling how he might react if Felkerson began rocking the boat. It didn't really make much difference, I thought. In twenty-four hours or so it would all be over.

"Drive carefully, Colonel," Campbell said when the RV was loaded. "Major McCauley and I will be at your place tomorrow afternoon. Then we have a date with destiny." Felkerson gave him a smart salute, climbed into the RV and drove off.

"Well, Major, I'm sure you'll want to clean up. Dinner will be served promptly at six o'clock. Just come right into the house whenever you're ready."

I went upstairs in the carriage house and found that the fatigue uniform I'd picked out had been laundered, ironed and laid out on the bed for me – Mary doing her part in her husband's mad scheme. I was thinking about her when Campbell called out from below.

"I have exactly five twenty-five and thirty seconds," he said. "Synchronize your watch."

I went along with his little game, marveling at his insanity and wondering what kind of demons were driving him. At the table he was a tightly coiled spring of restrained energy. Mary served us a roast beef dinner, then returned to the kitchen while we ate in private. The roast was well done, the general in rare form.

"Do you feel it, Major?" he asked, his eyes aglow. "Do you feel that sense of history in the making? We are fortunate, very fortunate. We have been called upon to change the course of events in this hemisphere, maybe to change the course of history. A few weeks from now it will be a whole new ballgame. We'll be engaged in a struggle to the death with the forces of evil. We'll be in the forefront of the battle to free mankind from Communist domination."

He had put his toupee aside, apparently for the duration, and his bald head glowed in the lamplight. His eyes were wild, alive with his perverted vision of the future, a heroic leader riding at the head of an avenging Christian army, charging to victory over the atheistic foe. What if he lost? I thought, wondering if there was room in his demented dream for a personal apocalypse. I ate, but with little appetite, and when we had finished he invited me to join him next door in the church.

"Together we'll pray for victory, Major. The Lord's hand has been on my shoulder from the beginning and it is time to ask His blessing on our endeavor. Come kneel with me before the Lord, Major, and feel the earth move with His righteous power."

"I tell you what, General, the Lord and I haven't exactly been on speaking terms for a long time. You do the praying. I don't want to do anything that might spoil your personal relationship with Him. You understand. I'll put my faith in your prayers and just go up and get a good night's sleep."

He nodded sagely, if a little sadly, and placed his hand on my shoulder, more in forgiveness than in understanding. Then we went our separate ways.

Chapter 22

I didn't turn on the lights, but stretched out on the bed in the shadows, wondering if I had been a fool to let things go this far. I'd got what I wanted to put my life back together again, why stick my neck out now? I was thinking about splitting right then and there when I saw her standing at the window, the moonlight falling full upon her – Mary Campbell, the voluptuous and probably very lonely Mary Campbell.

"You watching him pray?" I asked quietly.

"Yes," she said softly. "He does this every night. He's very religious."

"Is that what he is?" She knew exactly what I meant.

"He gets a little strange at times," she conceded. "He'll be over there for hours, praying and talking to himself. Look at him."

I came up behind her and peaked over her shoulder. Through the window of the chancel I could see him kneeling at the altar, his eyes uplifted, his hands clasped in prayer. It was warm in this garret and I could smell Mary's perfume, that same perfume I smelled in the snows of Alaska after nearly getting my head blown off. I also remembered the soft touch of her fingers on my throat that day as she felt for a pulse and I wanted to feel her touch again now. I put my arms around her waist and she turned her head slightly and tilted it back to be kissed. As we embraced I could see her breasts rise and fall beneath the sheerest of blouses. I noticed that she'd unbuttoned the first two buttons. I guided her over to the bed and helped with the rest of them. In a moment she was pressing my face against her bosom, just as she'd done that night in the cabin. She seemed to like that. I kissed her all over and she seemed to like that, too, liked it so much that she eased me onto the bed and returned the favor. She was the same hungry lover I remembered from our brief interlude, savoring every sensation. When we were ready at last she mounted me as if I were some magical horse and rode me rhythmically through the night and out of this world into a state of ecstasy. As she swayed over me I reached up and touched the rich softness of her. It was then I noticed the silver chain around her neck and the Omega charm that dangled from it, the same as the one Doctor Ross had used to try to hypnotize me. So she's one of them, I thought. Campbell might ignore her, but he'd put his mark on her and while he was off to seek his own fulfillment, she had come up here to seek hers. In time – glorious, unreckoned time – we found that fulfillment together only moments after Campbell found his. He burst through the door downstairs and shouted: "McCauley! I felt the hand of the Lord upon me! He's with us, McCauley. We go with the Lord's blessing!"

"Answer him," Mary whispered. "Answer him before he comes up here."

"That's fine, General, just fine," I stammered. "Uh, see you in the morning."

"Hallelujah!" he bellowed. "Hallelujah!"

Then the door slammed shut and it was so quiet I could hear Mary's heart beating slowly, steadily with an incredible calm, while my own was pounding erratically.

"That was close!" I gasped. "He'd kill us both, if he caught us like this. What's he going to think when he finds you're not in the house?"

"He won't know," she said. "My bedroom door is closed and he never comes near me, particularly when he's like this."

"You're sure?"

"He doesn't come near me, believe me. He never comes near me."

It was almost nine o'clock, but our evening had just begun. Mary seemed to be trying to make up for all she had missed over the years in her loveless marriage. Once as we

185

rested I watched that shiny little Omega charm riding on the gentle swells of her breast and remembered what the FBI had told me: Campbell had organized an Omega Force in every unit of The Group so that each had a combat capability, no matter how small it might be. It amused me to think that for all his organizational abilities, Campbell couldn't keep track of his own wife.

* * *

"Army surplus," Campbell explained as we pulled into the Felkersons' mountain property. He was referring to the two trucks and a Jeep that were parked in the driveway. A detail from Omega Force was busily transferring the arms and ammunition from Felkerson's RV into the trucks. The men were in full battle dress, their arms stacked on the close-clipped front lawn at the base of the flagpole. High overhead Old Glory flapped in a steady breeze and I wondered what the founding fathers who had invented that flag and fought and died to establish its primacy would make of all this. Felkerson greeted the general with a smart salute.

"We'll be ready to roll in an hour, sir," he reported.

"No hurry, Colonel," Campbell said. "We'll wait until evening after the commuter traffic has subsided. No use attracting any more attention than necessary. I've worked out this route using back roads whenever possible." He handed Felkerson a map and asked, "What time is the rendezvous?"

"The truck with the missiles is due at midnight, sir, the transport plane by 2 a.m. We'll have more than enough time if we leave here at 6:30. I've allowed an hour and a half to load the transport plane and we should be airborne by 4 a.m."

Campbell smiled benignly.

Each truck carried fifteen men, including a driver and co-driver. I was ordered to drive the Jeep, with Felkerson and the general as my passengers. I had plenty of time to study the map that afternoon and had the route committed to memory by chow time at five. The dour Mrs. Felkerson and her dutiful husband served up hamburgers, tossed salad and corn on the cob as if this were a Fourth of July picnic, and at precisely six-thirty Campbell gave the order to move out. Our little convoy rolled down the driveway and off into the dusk to whatever fate awaited us. Felkerson took the map and navigated for me as we skirted the heavily populated Silicon Valley and headed toward California's rich Central Valley. I knew from my study of the map that our rendezvous was a ranch south of Fresno, about as near to the middle of nowhere as one could get. As we approached each turning point, Felkerson switched on his flashlight and barked out the orders, "Left at the next junction, then south on County Road G." In between times I could see in the rear view mirror that he was whispering to Campbell. I wondered if he was making a last-minute pitch to dump me, but Campbell seemed distracted, nodding now and then but not responding. Finally I figured that if they planned to "terminate" me, it probably would be after we reached the ranch. Some five hours later we turned off a county road and after several miles I caught sight of the spread in the bright moonlight. I could make out a large, rambling home, a huge barn and a scattering of outbuildings.

"Stop here," Felkerson ordered as we reached the house. "Form the men up and stand by, Major. The general and I will be back shortly."

They headed toward the house and were met halfway by a tall, rangy man in a straw hat, jeans and cowboy boots. They spoke briefly while I ordered the men to dismount and form up in two ranks. In a moment Felkerson returned.

"Have your drivers follow my Jeep," he ordered. "We'll unload our gear at the edge of the airstrip."

"Yes, sir," I said with a snappy salute. I couldn't tell in the dark, but I was sure he was wearing what passed for a smile.

While the men worked, parallel lines of landing lights flicked on and off nearby, delineating the airstrip. It was a quick test to make sure everything was ready for H-Hour. Through the open doors of the barn I could see the blinking reds lights of a scanner and the shadowy outline of a radio operator monitoring the channels for the plane's approach signal. Several yards behind us Campbell called out, "Here comes our ordnance. Issue M16s and two clips of ammunition for each man, Major. Side arms for the officers. Stand by to unload that truck will all possible haste the moment it stops."

"Yes, sir."

The headlights of a large truck were coming our way along the dusty ranch road – the delivery boys of The Group carrying the Stinger missiles. The last of our gear was piled neatly at the edge of the airstrip when the truck came to a halt in a cloud of dust, its engine idling. The men scurried aboard and in fifteen minutes the truck was empty. Then its engines roared to life and the big van swung about and hurried back down the road away from the ranch. Moments later the crackling of radio transmissions could be heard from the barn. Campbell rushed out, shouting, "Stand by. Here she comes."

The landing lights blinked on, illuminating a graded and compacted airstrip, while in the distance I heard the first sound a plane's engines. In a matter of moments I could see its silvery nose just an instant before its landing gear touched down several hundred yards to the north. It was a DC-3 and had come in without landing lights. It taxied toward us and as the pilot feathered his engines the lights of the airstrip flicked off again and the plane came to a halt opposite us in the darkness.

"Stand fast," Campbell bellowed. "Are your men ready, Major."

I checked the formation, two ranks of men aligned with the row of crates and boxes of provisions.

"Yes, sir," I responded. "The men are ready."

As Campbell strode toward the plane its cargo door swung open and a small beam of light fell upon Campbell. He paused twenty yards from plane and called out, "Gen. Robert Campbell," to identify himself. Then two huge spotlights blinked on and raked the line of men and equipment at the edge of the landing strip. I saw Campbell throw up his hands to protect his eyes from the light while shouting, "Turn those damned things off! Turn them off!"

Felkerson sidled toward me, muttering, "Something's wrong here." I heard him slam a clip into his .45. Then a voice boomed from a loudspeaker aboard the plane.

"Stay where you are, all of you. This is the FBI and you are under arrest. I repeat, you are under arrest."

I saw Campbell pull his .45 and squeeze off two rounds before a hail of small arms fire cut him down. There was total confusion in the ranks. Most of the men turned and fled into the shadows out of the beam of the searchlights. Others ducked into the barn. Felkerson fell back a few paces, shouting to me, "It's a trap, you bastard. You set us up!" His first shot passed only inches from my head as I dove into the shadows. A couple of the men began firing volleys toward the plane, while I grabbed an M-16 leveled it on Felkerson just as he fired off another shot at me. I felt the burn as it ripped my fatigue jacket and grazed the flesh of my right side. I didn't give him a chance to fire again. I rose up on one knee and squeezed the trigger, firing off the whole clip. The blast cut him nearly in half. Suddenly a pickup truck wheeled out of the barn and raced toward us along the road. Campbell's cowboy conspirator wanted no part this ambush. I ripped a grenade from my belt and pulled the pin, letting the safety lever fly. The firing chain cooked for a couple of seconds before I chucked the grenade under the pickup as it raced by. The blast flung the truck off the road where it burst into flames. Suddenly our whole area was surrounded by government agents, their luminous vests identifying them as FBI and ATF. The remaining young men of Omega Force, their arms stretched skyward, surrendered without resistance.

"That's right," I told them, raising my own hands above my head. "They've got us. Let's not make it a massacre. Drop your weapons and keep our hands high."

"I don't get it, sir," said the sergeant. "What's going on?"

"The war's over, son," I said. "And we just got mustered out."

"Good job, McCauley," said a familiar voice behind me. It was young Evans, my buddy from the FBI.

"I'm glad to see you, Evans. You guys believe in cutting it close."

"It seemed the best way to round up the key people," he said. "And the evidence we'll need to convict them."

"How's Campbell?" I asked.

"Dead, I'm afraid."

"So is Felkerson. But you missed The Groupies who brought the Stingers awhile ago. They went thataway."

"We'll get them. We sealed road right after they drove in. What's this?" he asked, motioning toward the burning pickup.

"That was the cowboy who owns this layout. He was in a hurry to leave and I thought you might want to talk to him."

"We'll look after him. Say, it seems you got nicked. We'll have our medic look after you."

"Just a scratch," I said. "But I could use a ride home."

"Sure. That can be arranged," he smiled. "But you'll have to stay…"

"I know, stay close to my phone. Don't worry. I'm not going anywhere."

"I'd like to arrange something official to thank you for your help, Major. But unfortunately Washington tells me you don't exist."

"So I understand," I said with a grim smile. "How about a dash of sulfa powder and a Band-Aid and we'll call it even?"

"No problem, but if the government can help in any way…"

"Forget it. The government's done quite enough to me already. I'd be obliged if you feds just kept out of my life entirely."

"Why, McCauley, you're beginning to sound like these dissidents. You're liable to attract the wrong kind of friends, talking like that."

"There's only one person I'm interested in attracting right now, and she's a long way from here. If Uncle Sam really wants to help, how about that lift back to the city?"

* * *

I stayed close to my telephone for a few days, but the feds apparently didn't need my testimony to build a case against the illicit weekend warriors of Omega Force. And with Campbell, Felkerson and Peabody out of the way – and Ross on his way out, if he wasn't dead already – they had little to worry about. I tried to get a call through to Cindy Albright, but couldn't get an answer, so I decided to see if I could get the TR-3 running again. It had been a long time since I'd had the pleasure of getting grease up to my elbows. I needed a new pair of carburetors that weren't available locally, but I located them in a Moss Motors catalog and in a few days they arrived from Santa Barbara. By the time November rolled around I had the car humming and was ready to hit the road.

There was a lot of scenery between Cindy and me, some of the most beautiful at Cultus Lake in the Cascades of Central Oregon where I'd spent my honeymoon with Elizabeth a lifetime ago. I stopped there at the resort for a few days, just to reassure myself that once upon a time I had something to live for, that I was once a normal guy with a wife and a kid and a dream. But it was too much for me. Those memories that I'd worked so hard to restore were bringing me nothing but gloom. So before long I was back on the road, trying to convince myself that maybe I could do it all over again, even at my age, if Cindy was willing to take a gamble. I called her from Portland and this time I caught her at home. She answered with that throaty, seductive voice that made me hope that my daydreams weren't too far-fetched. She said to catch the ferry in Everett, Washington, and she'd meet me at the landing in Clinton on the south end of Whidbey Island. She was waiting at the dock when the boat pulled in, looking like a million dollars, all tanned and fresh and beautiful, just as I remembered her from our shipboard romance.

"Love your car, Pete!" she exclaimed. "How've you been?"

"If I were any happier I'd feel guilty. Great to see you again, Cindy. Hop in, or have you got a car here?"

"No. I had mother drive me down. It's a little chilly to drive with the top down, isn't it?"

"There's an old army blanket behind the seat. Bundle up and be my navigator. This is strange country to me." It would be even stranger, I thought, if Cindy's mother lived with her.

We followed the main road up the island to Coupeville and spent the rest of the afternoon as tourists in the quaint old village. After the sun had set we drove around the bend to The Captain Whidbey, a rustic inn, and sat by the fireplace in the lobby for cocktails. Later we got a window table in the dining room overlooking Penn Cove and enjoyed some of the best salmon I'd had since Skagway. We lingered over coffee and I noted there were rooms available upstairs, but Cindy had other plans.

"No, you've got to see my house," she said. "It's a lovely old Victorian. It's got a telephone, running water and a propane water heater, but that's about it when it comes to modern conveniences. You'll enjoy the view of the strait and we can build a fire to keep warm, which means you may have to split some wood."

"Sounds cozy," I said, "just you and me and your mother."

"No, silly. She doesn't live with me. She's got a mobile home in Oak Harbor. I may take her in later, but for now she wants to be alone. We just returned from Indiana – my father's funeral. She was going to stay, but I convinced her to come back with me, at least for a few months until she gets herself together."

"That was very good of you," I said, feeling ashamed for my gaffe about her mother. "Maybe we should be on our way, if I have to chop wood for a fire."

She did not exaggerate. It was a beautiful old house with gingerbread trim and gabled windows, standing foursquare against a gale wind that swept in off the Strait of San Juan de Fuca and bent the cypress trees that lined the cliff. Cindy, wrapped in my blanket, leaped from the car.

"Hurry," she cried. "Let's get a fire going before we freeze." I grabbed my bag from the car and followed her inside. "There's plenty of wood by the fireplace. See if you can get a fire going while I light the kerosene lamps."

"Kerosene lamps!"

"There's no electricity yet; it's next on my agenda. Besides," she said, flashing a gorgeous smile and growling, "I like to rough it."

I liked the way she said that, but then she could have said "It looks like rain" and I would have found it sexy. While I laid a fire and lit it, she fired up three lamps and used one to guide me upstairs with my bag to the spare bedroom, although she apparently had no intention of sleeping alone. Everything spelled romance – the blazing fire, the golden glow of the kerosene lamps, the wind making the house creak and groan. We snuggled on the couch for an hour or so, holding hands and talking softly, enjoying an occasional embrace, until the fire began to slowly fade to glowing embers.

"Sorry about your father," I said at one point. "I guess that's why I couldn't reach you."

"It's meant a lot of changes in my life, Pete. For one thing, I don't have to work anymore and I'm not at all sorry about that. There's a million things to do around an old place like this, and now at last I have the time and the money to do them."

193

"Had you thought about having a man around to handle the heavy jobs? I'm available, Cindy, and I would earn my keep."

"How do I know I could afford you?"

"I'd work for a smile and an occasional kind word, if they came from you."

"That's sweet, Pete. That'll be my name for you. Sweet Pete my handyman."

It was neither a yes or a no, but it was tender enough to lead to another kiss – and that led inevitably upstairs where we paused at the door to the spare bedroom, lighting our way with the kerosene lamps.

"You can change in here," she said, leaning close to me. "I'm going to take a shower. Whenever you're ready, come over to my room and make yourself comfortable. I won't be long."

It was an awkward kiss, what with each of us balancing a lamp, but it held a promise of wonderful things to come. I probably set a record for undressing in the icy room. The wind off the water gusted through the warped window frames and I was glad I'd brought a wool robe. I slipped into it before the chill cooled my ardor and padded down the hall to her bedroom. It was warmer there, away from the wind, and her windows were hung with heavy drapes. I poked idly about the room, holding my lamp high to examine the pictures on the wall, photographs of Cindy as a little girl, and a portrait of her taken for her high school graduation. Another showed her with a handsome young man, probably her late husband, Albright, the law student who had been wasted in Vietnam. He was a handsome kid, very serious, with brooding eyes and a sensitive mouth. What a shame they couldn't have had a life together. No wonder it had taken her so long to get over his death.

It heard the shower turn off and while she dried herself I continued looking around the room. Above the dresser was a sampler she must have done in grade school, a bit of embroidery signed Cindy F in large, clumsy letters across the bottom. Next to it was a framed snapshot of a pretty little girl on her father's lap. In her jewelry tray on the dresser top were the earrings she'd hastily removed, along with an opal ring and a silver chain with a small charm. It caught my eye because it looked familiar. I picked it up to examine it more closely and suddenly my blood ran cold. It was an Omega symbol. In a flash everything came rushing together to form a chilling picture – Cindy aboard the Stardancer where I'd had a close brush with death; Cindy caring for a newly widowed mother. It all fit. I lifted the lamp to take a closer look at the snapshot of the little girl and her father. It was the young Harold Felkerson. The Cindy F of the childhood sampler was Cindy Felkerson! That's where the money came from to renovate this old house – the Felkersons' hideaway in the Santa Cruz Mountains must have been worth a million or more. And here she was now with everything she could want in life, including the guy who'd gunned down her father only a few weeks ago with a burst from an M16.

I could hear her humming softly in the bathroom as she toweled off her beautiful body. I could see every line of it in my imagination and I longed to hold her close to me and feel her warm skin against mine. I didn't want to believe what I knew must be true. I had waited so long for this moment, only to find myself torn between a deep desire and a rising panic that screamed in my ears, "Run, you fool, run!" But before I could move a muscle the bathroom door swung open and the first thing to emerge was the muzzle of a snub-nosed .38 caliber revolver. Our eyes met for only a split second, but that was long enough to read the hate that burned in her eyes, hate that twisted her lips in a grin of perverse pleasure now that the object of her animosity stood only ten feet away, naked to her deadly retribution. My reaction was only an instant faster than hers. I flung the kerosene lamp in her direction just as she squeezed the trigger. The slug slammed into the dresser just as the lamp smashed against the wall behind her, showering her with liquid fire. With a shriek her blazing form flashed by me and out the door, spreading flames as she careened down the hall. The .38 went off again as she collided with the banister, spun about and plunged down the stairs. I raced after her and stood aghast at the writhing inferno that lay at my feet. Her eyes were open and she seemed to be staring at me from the depths of hell. I snatched my blanket from the couch and turned to smother the flames – but it was too late. I wrapped the blanket around me and stumbled out into the frigid air just as the windows shattered and the house exploded in flames. I could do nothing but stare in horror as the wind-whipped fire devoured the place. Then in the distance I heard the eerie wail of a siren responding to the blood-red glow in the night sky.